Graphic Classics:
MARK TWAIN

Graphic Classics Volume Eight

2004

EUREKA PRODUCTIONS

8778 Oak Gr   nsin 53572

D1533816

" .. LIFE ITSELF IS ONLY A VISION .. A DREAM .. "

from THE MYSTERIOUS STRANGER ©2004 DAN O'NEILL

CONTENTS

Graphic Classics:
MARK TWAIN

Cover illustration by George Sellas / Back cover illustration by Evert Geradts
Additional illustrations by Dan O'Neill, Kevin Atkinson, William L. Brown and George Sellas

Graphic Classics: Mark Twain is published by Eureka Productions. ISBN #0-9712464-8-3. Price US $9.95. Available from Eureka Productions, 8778 Oak Grove Road, Mount Horeb, WI 53572. The Graphic Classics website is at http://www.graphicclassics.com. Tom Pomplun, designer and publisher, tom@graphicclassics.com. Eileen Fitzgerald, editorial assistant. This compilation and all original works ©2004 Eureka Productions. All rights revert to creators after publication. Graphic Classics is a trademark of Eureka Productions. Printed in Canada. *Illustration* ©2004 WILLIAM L. BROWN

SEVENTIETH BIRTHDAY

by **MARK TWAIN**

illustrated by **MARK DANCEY**

Excerpted from an address at a dinner at Delmonico's, December 5, 1905, to celebrate the seventieth anniversary of Mr. Clemens' Birth.

I HAVE HAD A GREAT MANY BIRTHDAYS in my time. I remember the first one very well, and I always think of it with indignation; everything was so crude, unaesthetic, primeval. Nothing like this at all.

This is my seventieth birthday, and I wonder if you all rise to the size of that proposition, realizing all the significance of that phrase, seventieth birthday.

It is the time of life when you arrive at a new and awful dignity; when you may throw aside the decent reserves which have oppressed you for a generation and stand unafraid and unabashed upon your seven-terraced summit and look down and teach – unrebuked. You shall never get tired of telling by what delicate arts and deep moralities you climbed up to that great place. You will explain the process and dwell on the particulars with senile rapture. I have been anxious to explain my own system this long time, and now at last I have the right.

I have achieved my seventy years in the usual way: by sticking strictly to a scheme of life which would kill anybody else. It sounds like an exaggeration, but that is really the common rule for attaining to old age. I will offer here, as a sound maxim, this: That we can't reach old age by another man's road.

I will now teach, offering my way of life to whomsoever desires to commit suicide by the scheme which has enabled me to beat the doctor and the hangman for seventy years.

We have no permanent habits until we are forty. Then they begin to harden, presently they petrify, then business begins. Since forty I have been regular about going to bed and getting up—and that is one of the main things. I have made it a rule to go to bed when there wasn't anybody left to sit up with; and I have made it a rule to get up when I had to. This has resulted in an unswerving regularity of irregularity. It has saved me sound, but it would injure another person.

In the matter of diet—which is another main thing—I have been persistently strict in sticking to the things which didn't agree with me until one or the other of us got the best of it. Until lately I got the best of it myself. But last spring I stopped frolicking with mince-pie after midnight; up to then I had always believed it wasn't loaded. For thirty years I have taken coffee and bread at eight in the morning, and no bite nor sup until seven-thirty in the evening. Eleven hours. That is all right for me, and is wholesome, because I have never had a headache in my life, but headachy people would not reach seventy comfortably by that road, and they would be foolish to try it.

I have made it a rule never to smoke more than one cigar at a time. I have no other restriction as regards smoking. As an example to others, and not that I care for moderation myself, it has always been my rule never to smoke when asleep, and never to refrain when awake.

As for drinking, I have no rule about that. When the others drink I like to help; otherwise I remain dry, by habit and preference. This dryness does not hurt me, but it could easily hurt you, because you are different. You let it alone.

I have never taken any exercise, except sleeping and resting, and I never intend to take any. Exercise is loathsome. And it cannot be any benefit when you are tired; and I was always tired. But let another person try my way, and see where he will come out.

Threescore years and ten!

It is the Scriptural statute of limitations. After that, you owe no active duties; for you the strenuous life is over. You have served your term, well or less well, and you are mustered out. You are emancipated, compulsions are not for you, nor any bugle-call but "lights out." You pay the time-worn duty bills if you choose, or decline if you prefer—and without prejudice —for they are not legally collectable.

The previous-engagement plea, which in forty years has cost you so many twinges, you can lay aside forever; on this side of the grave you will never need it again. You need only reply, "Your invitation honors me, and pleases me because you still keep me in your remembrance, but I am seventy; seventy, and would nestle in the chimney-corner, and smoke my pipe, and read my book, and take my rest, wishing you well in all affection, and that when you in your return shall arrive at pier No. 70 you may step aboard your waiting ship with a reconciled spirit, and lay your course toward the sinking sun with a contented heart."

The Mysterious Stranger

*by **Mark Twain***
*adapted & illustrated by **Rick Geary***

It was 1590. It was still the Middle Ages in Austria, and promised to remain so forever.

Our village drowsed in a woodsy solitude, where news of the outside world hardly ever disturbed its dreams.

The whole region was the hereditary property of a prince, whose servants kept the castle in perfect condition, though he rarely visited there.

Eseldorf was a paradise for us boys. We were not overmuch pestered with schooling. Knowledge was not good for the common people, and could make them discontented with the lot which God had appointed for them.

We had two priests. Father Adolf was held in more solemn respect, because he had no fear at all of the Devil. This was known to be so, since Father Adolf had said it himself.

But it was Father Peter, the other priest, that we all loved best. But some people charged him with saying that God was all goodness and would find a way to save all his children.

It was a horrible thing to say, but there was never any proof that he had actually said it.

Father Peter had an enemy, and a very powerful one, the astrologer who lived in an old tower up the valley, and put in his nights studying the stars.

Everyone knew he could foretell wars and famines, though that was not so hard, for there was always a war, and generally a famine somewhere.

Everyone in the village except Father Peter stood in awe of him.

Father Peter denounced the astrologer openly as a charlatan, which made the astrologer hate Father Peter and wish to ruin him.

It was the astrologer, as we all believed, who originated the story about Father Peter's shocking remark and carried it to the bishop. The bishop suspended Father Peter indefinitely, though he wouldn't go so far as to excommunicate him.

Those had been hard years for the old priest and his niece, Marget. Many of their friends fell away entirely, and the rest became cool and distant.

Marget was a lovely girl of eighteen when the trouble came, and she had the best head in the village. She taught the harp, but her scholars fell off one by one.

The young fellows also stopped coming to the house, all except Wilhelm Meidling, who remained loyal.

Matters went worse and worse, all through the two years. And now, at last, the very end was come. Solomon Isaacs, the banker, gave notice that tomorrow he would foreclose on the house.

Three of us boys were always together, and had been so from the cradle –

Nikolaus Bauman, son of the local judge.

Seppi Wohlmeyer, son of the innkeeper.

And I was the third – Theodor Fischer.

We knew the hills and the woods and were always roaming them when we had leisure. One May morning we went up into the hills, and there we stretched out on the grass in the shade to rest and smoke and talk.

Soon there came a youth strolling toward us through the trees.

He sat down and began to talk in a friendly way, just as if he knew us. He was handsome, and wore new clothes.

I offered our pipe to him, but then I remembered that we had no fire.

FIRE? OH, I WILL FURNISH IT.

I was astonished, for I had not said anything.

He took the pipe and blew on it.

9

We jumped up and were going to run, but he pleaded with us to stay, giving his word that he only wanted to be friends with us.

He was bent on putting us at ease, and before long we were comfortable and chatty. He said such tricks came natural to him.

LET US SEE ANOTHER!

WITH PLEASURE.

He said he would give us any kind of fruit we liked, whether it was in season or not.

ORANGE!

APPLE!

GRAPES!

THEY ARE IN YOUR POCKETS,

AND EVERYTHING ELSE YOUR APPETITES CALL FOR— AS LONG AS I AM WITH YOU, YOU HAVE ONLY TO WISH.

He did one curious thing after another to amuse us.

He made a tiny squirrel out of clay, and it ran up a tree.

Then he made a toy dog that barked at the squirrel.

He made clay birds and they flew away, singing.

At last I asked him to tell us who he was.

AN ANGEL.

A kind of awe fell upon us, but he said we need not be afraid of an angel.

He went on chatting, and while he talked he made a crowd of little men and women, no bigger than your finger.

They went diligently to work and cleared a space in the grass and began to build a little castle.

Five hundred of these toy people swarming about and wiping the sweat off their faces as natural as life.

TELL US— WHAT IS YOUR NAME?

SATAN.

The name caught us suddenly, and we drew back from him.

THAT SEEMS A STRANGE NAME FOR AN ANGEL.

WHY?

BECAUSE— WELL, IT'S HIS NAME.

OH, YES— HE IS MY UNCLE.

HE IS THE ONLY MEMBER OF OUR FAMILY THAT HAS EVER SINNED.

Satan read the question bursting in my mind.

HAVE I SEEN HIM? MILLIONS OF TIMES. FROM WHEN I WAS A LITTLE CHILD, UNTIL THE FALL, I WAS HIS FAVORITE. FOR EIGHT THOUSAND YEARS, AS YOU COUNT TIME.

EIGHT...THOUSAND! BUT YOU SEEM A BOY, LIKE US.

WHY, NATURALLY. A BOY IS WHAT I AM. WITH US, TIME IS A SPACIOUS THING.

I AM SIXTEEN THOUSAND YEARS OLD. THE FALL DID NOT AFFECT ME. WE OTHERS ARE STILL IGNORANT OF SIN—

He was interrupted by two of the little workmen, who were quarreling. In buzzing little voices they were cursing each other.

Satan reached out his hand and crushed the life out of them with his fingers.

We were shocked at the murder he had committed.

But he went right on talking, as if nothing had happened.

WE ANGELS CAN DO NO WRONG, FOR WE KNOW NOT WHAT IT IS.

Now the wives of the little dead men had found the crushed bodies and were crying over them.

Satan paid no attention until the noise of the weeping and praying began to annoy him.

Then he reached out and took the heavy board seat out of our swing and mashed all those people into the earth just as if they had been flies!

It made us sick to see that awful deed.

But he went on talking right along, and worked his enchantments on us. He made us forget everything, and we could only listen and love him.

The Stranger had been everywhere, he had seen everything, and he forgot nothing. He had seen the world made; he had seen Adam created; he had seen the damned writhing in hell; and he made us see all these things.

He told us his real name was to be known to us alone. He had chosen another one to be called by in the presence of others – Philip Traum.

We had seen wonders this day; and my thoughts began to run on the pleasure it would be to tell of them.

NO, THESE MATTERS ARE A SECRET AMONG US. I WILL PROTECT YOUR TONGUES, AND NOTHING WILL ESCAPE.

FATHER PETER IS COMING. SIT STILL, AND BE QUIET.

I CAN'T THINK WHY I AM HERE; I WAS IN MY STUDY A MINUTE AGO — BUT I AM NOT MYSELF THESE DAYS.

He walked straight through Satan, just as if nothing were there.

I TOLD YOU — I AM BUT A SPIRIT.

Then he chatted along the same as ever. He spoke of men in the same way that one speaks of bricks and manure piles. I asked what was the difference between men and himself.

THE DIFFERENCE? MAN IS MADE OF DIRT. HE COMES TODAY AND IS GONE TOMORROW.

AND MAN HAS THE MORAL SENSE. THAT IS ENOUGH DIFFERENCE BETWEEN US, ALL BY ITSELF.

I had a dim idea of what the Moral Sense was. But I knew that we were proud of it.

I AM GOING NOW, BUT I WILL BE BACK.

Then he vanished.

I SUPPOSE NONE OF IT HAPPENED.

It was the same fear that was in my own mind. Then we saw Father Peter wandering back.

MAYBE YOU BOYS CAN HELP ME. I HAVE LOST MY WALLET. IT WAS ALL THAT I HAD.

WE WILL HELP LOOK.

HERE IT IS!

There it lay, right where Satan had vanished.

IT IS MINE, BUT NOT THESE. WHO HAS BEEN HERE?

The wallet was stuffed full with gold coins.

We all tried to say "Satan did it!" But we couldn't say his name.

NO HUMAN BEING.

WE SAW NO MAN.

IT'S ELEVEN HUNDRED DUCATS! IF IT WERE ONLY MINE—I NEED IT SO!

IT IS YOURS, SIR!

NO—IT ISN'T MINE. ONLY FOUR DUCATS.

WE ARE WITNESSES, FATHER PETER.

WE'LL STAND BY IT, TOO.

BLESS YOUR HEARTS, YOU ALMOST PERSUADE ME. IF I HAD ONLY A HUNDRED-ODD DUCATS OF IT...

IT'S YOURS, ALL OF IT, AND YOU MUST TAKE IT.

Finally, he said he would use two hundred of it, to save his house, and would put the rest at interest until the rightful owner came for it.

And we boys must sign a paper to prove that he had not got out of his troubles dishonestly.

It made much talk when Father Peter paid the mortgage in gold.

There was a pleasant change, and many old friends called at the house to congratulate him.

The old priest told the story just as it had happened, and said he could not account for it, only it was the hand of Providence.

One or two shook their heads and said privately it looked more like the hand of Satan, and tried to coax us boys to come out and "tell the truth."

There was a question which we wanted to ask Father Peter.

WHAT IS THE MORAL SENSE?

WHY, IT IS THE FACULTY WHICH ENABLES US TO TELL GOOD FROM EVIL.

IS IT VALUABLE?

VALUABLE?! IT IS THE ONE THING THAT LIFTS MAN ABOVE THE BEASTS AND MAKES HIM HEIR TO IMMORTALITY!

We passed through the parlor, and there was Marget, teaching Marie Lueger. Other pupils would follow.

And in the garden, Wilhelm Meidling waited. The young lawyer's faithfulness was not lost on Marget and her uncle.

On the fourth day came the astrologer from his crumbling old tower and had a private talk with us.

HOW MANY DUCATS WAS IT?

ELEVEN HUNDRED.

A CURIOUS COINCIDENCE. I KNOW THE THIEF NOW. THE MONEY WAS STOLEN.

Then he went away, leaving us wondering what he could mean.

In about an hour we found out; for it was all over the village that Father Peter had been arrested for stealing a great sum of money from the astrologer.

Many said it must be a mistake; but the others shook their heads and said misery and want could drive a man to almost anything.

Our characters began to suffer now. We were Father Peter's only witnesses; how much did he pay us to back up his fantastic tale?

Our fathers said we were disgracing our families, and our mothers begged us to save our families from shame.

We tried to tell the whole thing, Satan and all — but it wouldn't come out.

Father Peter was in prison, and the court would not sit for some time to come.

So Marget's new happiness died a quick death. There would be no scholars paying for lessons.

Ursula, who was housekeeper, said God would provide. But she meant to help in the providing.

On the fourth day after the catastrophe, I was out walking when a tingling sensation went rippling through me, and I knew that Satan was nearby.

Next moment he was alongside of me and I told him what had been happening to Marget and her uncle.

We saw Ursula resting in the shade of a tree, and she had a stray kitten in her lap.

I asked her where she got it.

IT CAME OUT OF THE WOODS AND FOLLOWED ME. I SUPPOSE I MUST LET IT GO, THOUGH IT WOULD BE SUCH PLEASANT COMPANY.

YOU SHOULD KEEP IT. THIS BREED BRINGS LUCK.

IS IT TRUE?

WELL, IT BRINGS MONEY, ANYWAY.

MONEY? PEOPLE DO NOT BUY CATS; ONE CAN'T GIVE THEM AWAY.

I DON'T MEAN SELL IT. THIS IS A LUCKY CAT. ITS OWNER FINDS FOUR SILVER GROSCHEN IN HIS POCKET EVERY MORNING.

I saw the indignation rising in Ursula's face. This boy was making fun of her. She thrust her hands into her pockets.

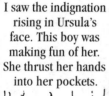

IT'S TRUE— IT'S TRUE!

Ursula started home-ward, with the kitten in her arms.

I said I wished I had her privilege of seeing Marget.

Then I caught my breath, for we were there in the parlor, and Marget looking at us, astonished.

I introduced Satan— that is, Philip Traum— and we were soon friends.

Marget couldn't keep her eyes off him, he was so beautiful.

He said he was an orphan, but he had a wealthy uncle in business down in the tropics.

I HOPE OUR UNCLES MEET SOME DAY.

I HOPE SO, TOO.

The possibility made me shudder, but they chatted on, and poor Marget forgot her sorrow for a little while.

He promised to get her admitted to the jail to visit her uncle.

ALWAYS GO IN THE EVENING AFTER DARK, AND SHOW THIS PAPER AS YOU PASS IN.

I judged that the marks on the paper were an enchantment, and that the guards would not know what they were doing, nor remember afterward.

Ursula entered to announce supper.

Then she saw us and looked frightened, and motioned me to come.

HAVE YOU TOLD MISS MARGET ABOUT THE CAT?

NO, WE HAVEN'T.

PLEASE DON'T; FOR SHE WOULD THINK IT UNHOLY, AND SEND FOR A PRIEST.

I was beginning to say goodbye to Marget, but Satan interrupted and ever so politely invited himself to supper, and me, too.

Marget was embarrassed, for she knew they did not have enough, and Ursula seemed not a bit pleased.

I TOLD YOU, IT IS A LUCKY CAT. IT WILL PROVIDE.

And so it did: an abundance of fish and game and wines and fruits; and Satan talked right along and made the time pass pleasantly.

When it was dark, Marget took food and wine in a basket and hurried to the jail.

I was thinking that I should like to see what the inside of the jail was like. Satan heard the thought, and the next moment we were in the torture chamber. The people there took no notice of us, as we were invisible.

A young man lay bound, and Satan said he was suspected of being a heretic.

CONFESS TO THE CHARGE!

BUT IT IS NOT TRUE!

Then they drove splinters under his nails, and he shrieked with the pain. I could not endure it.

WHAT A BRUTAL THING!

NO, IT WAS A HUMAN THING. ONLY MAN INFLICTS PAIN FOR THE PLEASURE OF INFLICTING IT, INSPIRED BY THAT MORAL SENSE OF HIS!

I WILL SHOW YOU MORE.

In a moment we were in a French village. We walked through a great factory, where men and women and little children were toiling.

THE PROPRIETORS ARE RICH, BUT THE WAGE THEY PAY IS ONLY ENOUGH TO KEEP THESE PEOPLE FROM DROPPING DEAD WITH HUNGER.

YOU HAVE SEEN HOW THEY TREAT A MISDOER THERE IN THE JAIL; NOW YOU SEE HOW THEY TREAT THE INNOCENT.

IT IS THE MORAL SENSE WHICH TEACHES THE OWNERS THE DIFFERENCE BETWEEN RIGHT AND WRONG—YOU PERCEIVE THE RESULT.

Then he overstrained himself making fun of us, and deriding our pride in our great heroes and our venerable history.

BUT, AFTER ALL, THERE IS A SORT OF PATHOS ABOUT IT WHEN ONE REMEMBERS HOW FEW ARE YOUR DAYS.

The next moment we were back in our village. I heard a joyful cry: It was Seppi Wohlmeyer.

YOU'VE COME AGAIN!

Seppi was full of the latest mystery– the disappearance of Hans Oppert, the village loafer.

NO ONE HAS SEEN HIM SINCE HE DID THAT BRUTAL THING.

WHAT THING?

WELL, HE WAS ALWAYS CLUBBING HIS DOG, AND TWO DAYS AGO HE STRUCK THE DOG WITH ALL HIS MIGHT AND KNOCKED ONE OF HIS EYES OUT. AND THEN HE LAUGHED, THE HEARTLESS BRUTE.

THERE IS THAT WORD AGAIN. BRUTES DO NOT ACT LIKE THAT, ONLY MEN.

Soon that poor dog came along, with his eye hanging down. It went straight to Satan and began to moan, and Satan answered, and it was plain that they were talking together in the dog language. Satan took the dog's head in his lap and put the eye back in its place, and the dog wagged his tail and licked Satan's hand.

HE SAYS HIS MASTER WAS DRUNK, AND HE FELL OVER A CLIFF.

THE DOG HAS BEEN BEGGING FOR HELP, BUT HE WAS ONLY DRIVEN AWAY. HE ONLY WANTED TO AID THE MAN WHO HAS MISTREATED HIM.

IS HEAVEN RESERVED FOR YOUR RACE, AND THIS DOG RULED OUT, AS YOUR TEACHERS TELL YOU?

We got some men and found the body. Nobody cared but the dog. He licked the dead face and could not be comforted.

There was a very dull week, now, for Satan did not come, and our parents forbade us to see Marget.

But we saw Ursula a couple of times. She bore a prosperous look.

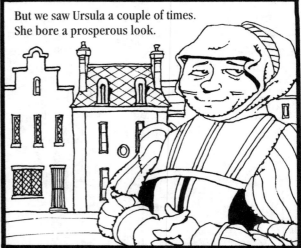

She said Marget spent an hour or two every night in the jail, and was enduring her isolation fairly well, with the help of Wilhelm Meidling.

The astrologer reported Marget and Ursula's new prosperity to Father Adolf.

THERE MUST BE WITCHCRAFT AT THE BOTTOM OF IT.

The priest told the villagers to resume relations with Marget and report to him.

YOU WILL BE UNDER MY PROTECTION FROM EVIL.

And so poor Marget began to have company again. The cat began to strain itself, providing for all the visitors.

Marget knew that nothing was impossible to Providence, but she could not help doubting that this effort was from there.

Marget announced a party, and invited forty people. The guests filled the place. Father Adolf arrived, and soon after him, the astrologer, without invitation.

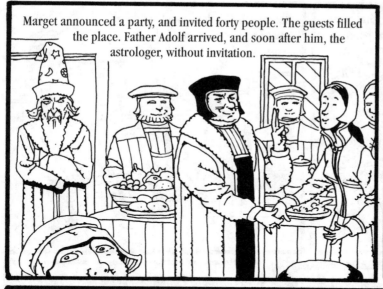

Satan came, as well.

He apologized for intruding, but Marget brought him in and introduced him to the guests.

There was quite a rustle of whispers among the girls.

The astrologer had drunk his second beaker of wine and poured out a third. when he noticed something.

He called for a large bowl and began to pour wine into it. He poured until the bowl was filled to the brim.

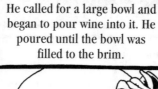

Yet the bottle remained full!

Father Adolf rose up, excited.

THIS HOUSE IS ACCURSED! I SUMMON THIS DETECTED HOUSEHOLD TO —

His words were cut short. His face became red, then purple, but he could not utter another sound.

The people began to cry and shriek and crowd toward the door.

Then I saw Satan melt into the astrologer's body.

WAIT — DON'T RUN!

He called for a funnel.

Then he took up the great bowl and poured all the wine back into the bottle.

IT IS NOTHING — WITH MY POWERS I CAN DO MUCH MORE!

MY GOD, HE IS POSSESSED!

The astrologer then strode from the house, as the crowd followed him at a distance.

When he reached the market square he went up to a juggler.

THIS CLOWN IS IGNORANT OF HIS ART. WATCH AN EXPERT PERFORM.

So saying, he tossed the balls up and set them whirling in the air.

He added another, and another, his hands moving so swiftly that they were just a blur.

Then he turned and saw the tightrope, and said now the people should see the work of a master.

He sprang into the air and lit on the tightrope. He hopped the length of it on one foot, then began to throw somersaults.

Finally he sprang lightly down and disappeared up the road.

WAS IT REAL?

OR WAS IT ALL A DREAM?

I returned to Marget's house, where it was like a funeral.

I HAVE BEEN BEGGING HIM TO GO, AND SO SAVE HIMSELF.

I WILL NOT GO. IF THERE IS DANGER, MY PLACE IS BY YOU.

There was a knock, and Satan came in and changed the mood.

He said not a word about what had happened, but instead rattled on about all manner of pleasant things.

Marget was charmed, but Wilhelm did not look pleased.

Late that night, Satan roused me from sleep.

WHERE SHALL WE GO?

ANYWHERE.

There was a fierce glare of sunlight, and we were over a strange land.

THIS IS CHINA.

I was drunk with vanity to think I had come so much farther than anybody else in our village.

Finally, we lit upon a mountaintop. As we talked, I had the idea of trying to reform Satan.

I KNOW YOU DO NOT MEAN ANY HARM, BUT YOU OUGHT TO STOP AND CONSIDER THE CONSEQUENCES OF A THING BEFORE DOING IT.

BUT I KNOW WHAT THE CONSEQUENCES ARE GOING TO BE — ALWAYS.

THEN HOW CAN YOU DO THESE THINGS?

WELL, YOU MUST UNDERSTAND IF YOU CAN.

MEN HAVE NOTHING IN COMMON WITH ME. MY MIND CREATES ANYTHING IT DESIRES — AND IN A MOMENT.

WE ANGELS CANNOT LOVE MEN, BUT WE CAN LIKE THEM. AND FOR YOUR SAKE I AM DOING THESE THINGS FOR THE VILLAGERS.

He saw that I was thinking a sarcasm, and he explained.

WHAT I AM DOING FOR THE VILLAGERS WILL BEAR GOOD FRUIT TO UNBORN GENERATIONS OF MEN.

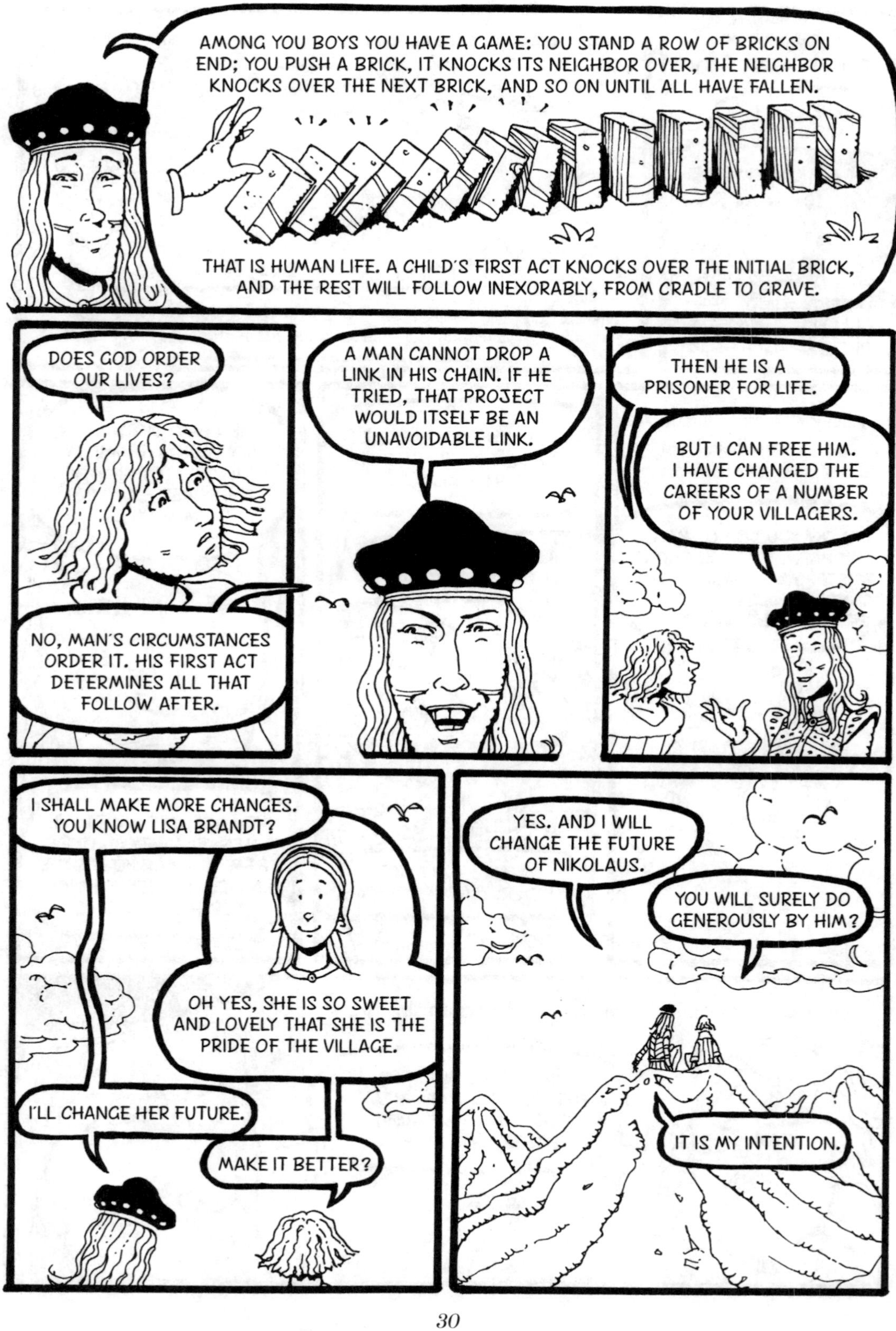
AMONG YOU BOYS YOU HAVE A GAME: YOU STAND A ROW OF BRICKS ON END; YOU PUSH A BRICK, IT KNOCKS ITS NEIGHBOR OVER, THE NEIGHBOR KNOCKS OVER THE NEXT BRICK, AND SO ON UNTIL ALL HAVE FALLEN.
THAT IS HUMAN LIFE. A CHILD'S FIRST ACT KNOCKS OVER THE INITIAL BRICK, AND THE REST WILL FOLLOW INEXORABLY, FROM CRADLE TO GRAVE.
DOES GOD ORDER OUR LIVES?
NO, MAN'S CIRCUMSTANCES ORDER IT. HIS FIRST ACT DETERMINES ALL THAT FOLLOW AFTER.
A MAN CANNOT DROP A LINK IN HIS CHAIN. IF HE TRIED, THAT PROJECT WOULD ITSELF BE AN UNAVOIDABLE LINK.
THEN HE IS A PRISONER FOR LIFE.
BUT I CAN FREE HIM. I HAVE CHANGED THE CAREERS OF A NUMBER OF YOUR VILLAGERS.
I SHALL MAKE MORE CHANGES. YOU KNOW LISA BRANDT?
OH YES, SHE IS SO SWEET AND LOVELY THAT SHE IS THE PRIDE OF THE VILLAGE.
I'LL CHANGE HER FUTURE.
MAKE IT BETTER?
YES. AND I WILL CHANGE THE FUTURE OF NIKOLAUS.
YOU WILL SURELY DO GENEROUSLY BY HIM?
IT IS MY INTENTION.

It made me feel creepy to hear him say that.

31

I wondered about poor little Lisa's fate.

SHE ESCAPES TEN YEARS OF PAINFUL RECOVERY, THEN NINETEEN OF SHAME AND DEPRAVITY, ENDING WITH DEATH AT THE HANDS OF THE EXECUTIONER.

PLEASE, NO.

BUT I CAN HELP FATHER PETER. HE WILL BE ACQUITTED, HIS GOOD NAME RESTORED, AND THE REST OF HIS LIFE WILL BE HAPPY.

That reminded me of the astrologer, and I wondered where he might be.

ON THE MOON. I'VE GOT HIM ON THE COLD SIDE OF IT, TOO. BUT I AM QUITE WILLING TO DO HIM A KINDNESS — I THINK I SHALL GET HIM BURNED.

He had a strange notion of kindness! But the ways of angels are not ours.

Satan returned me to my bed, but sleep would not come. My mind was filled with Nikolaus, and our days together.

In the morning I sought out Seppi and told him.

LESS THAN TWELVE DAYS?

We walked up among the hills and talked about our times with Nikolaus.

WE MUST BE WITH HIM ALL THE TIME; THESE DAYS ARE PRECIOUS.

It was a shock when we turned a curve and came upon Nikolaus face to face.

YOU LOOK LIKE YOU'VE SEEN A GHOST!

We wandered with him for many a mile, as we talked about old times.

Our tone toward him was so gentle that he noticed it, and was pleased.

We spent all of our spare time with Nikolaus. He was happy, but always puzzled because we were not.

When the evening of the last day came we stayed out too long. Seppi and I were in fault for that, for we could not bear to part with our friend.

In the morning, we went to his home. His mother met us at the door.

HIS FATHER IS OUT OF PATIENCE WITH THESE GOINGS-ON. NICKY GOT A FLOGGING FOR BEING LATE LAST NIGHT.

I AM SORRY, BUT HE CANNOT GO OUT OF THE HOUSE TODAY.

We had a great hope. If he could not leave the house, he could not be drowned!

She allowed us to go upstairs to visit Nikolaus.

We both noticed the time— a quarter to ten. Only such a few minutes to live!

SIT DOWN. I'VE FINISHED A KITE THAT IS DRYING IN THE KITCHEN. I'LL FETCH IT.

Then he went clattering down the stairs, as we sat and watched the clock.

THEODOR, HE WILL BE SAVED!

Then his mother entered, bringing the kite.

BUT WHERE IS NICKY?

HE'LL BE HERE SOON; HE'S OUT FOR A MINUTE.

HE'S OUTSIDE?

YES. LITTLE LISA'S MOTHER CAME IN AND SAID THE CHILD HAD WANDERED OFF SOME-WHERE. I TOLD NIKOLAUS TO GO OUT AND LOOK FOR HER.

We hurried to the window and looked toward the river.

IT IS ALL OVER! POOR NIKOLAUS!

Presently the thing happened which we were dreading. A crowd came solemnly in, and laid the two drowned bodies on the bed.

OH, IF ONLY I HAD KEPT HIM IN THE HOUSE, THIS WOULD NOT HAVE HAPPENED!

We heard screams, and Frau Brandt came wildly plunging through the crowd.

FOR TWO WEEKS I HAVE HAD DREAMS THAT DEATH WOULD STRIKE THAT MOST PRECIOUS TO ME.

AND DAY AND NIGHT I HAVE GROVELED IN THE DIRT, PRAYING FOR HIS PITY— AND HERE IS HIS ANSWER. I WILL NEVER PRAY AGAIN!

Both funerals took place the next day.

Everybody was there, even Satan; which was proper, for it was on account of him that the funerals had happened.

At the graveyard, the body of little Lisa was seized for debt by a carpenter to whom the mother owed fifty groschen.

He took the corpse home and kept it four days, then he buried it without ceremony in his brother's cattle-yard.

This drove the mother wild with grief and shame, and it was pitiful to see.

We begged Satan to examine the woman's possible careers, and see if he could not change her to a new one.

HER PATH IS CHARGED WITH GRIEF AND PAIN. THE ONLY IMPROVEMENT I COULD MAKE WOULD BE A CERTAIN THREE MINUTES FROM NOW.

DO IT!

IT IS DONE.

SHE IS NOW HAVING WORDS WITH FISCHER, THE WEAVER. IN HIS ANGER HE WILL BETRAY HER FOR THE BLASPHEMIES SHE SAID OVER HER CHILD'S BODY. IN THREE DAYS SHE WILL GO TO THE STAKE.

We were frozen with horror. Satan could not seem to do any person a kindness but by killing him.

BUT BY THIS PROMPT DEATH THE WOMAN GETS TWENTY-NINE YEARS MORE OF HEAVEN AND ESCAPES TWENTY-NINE YEARS OF MISERY HERE.

The trial was crowded. Frau Brandt's was easily convicted of her blas-phemies, for she said she would not take them back.

TAKE MY LIFE, AND WELCOME! I WOULD RATHER LIVE WITH THE REAL DEVILS IN PERDITION THAN WITH YOU IMITATORS.

They found her guilty, and she was sentenced and excommunicated.

We saw her chained to the stake, and we walked away and did not see the fires consume her, but we heard the shrieks.

When they ceased we knew she was in heaven, notwithstanding the excommunication; and we were not sorry that we had caused her death.

One day, a little while after this, Satan appeared again at the place where we had first met him. We asked him to do a show for us.

I WILL SHOW YOU THE PROGRESS OF HUMAN CIVILIZATION.

He showed us the Garden of Eden, and Cain's murder of Abel.

The vision was followed by a long series of wars, murders, massacres and hideous drenchings of blood.

We saw Caesar invade Britain.

HE WANTED TO CONFER THE BLESSINGS OF CIVILIZATION ON THE WIDOWS AND ORPHANS.

YOU HAVE MADE CONTINUAL PROGRESS. CAIN DID HIS MURDER WITH A CLUB; THE ROMANS WITH SWORDS; THE CHRISTIAN HAS ADDED GUNS.

WITHOUT CHRISTIAN CIVILIZATION, WAR MUST HAVE REMAINED A TRIFLING THING.

We saw Christianity and Civilization march hand in hand through the ages, leaving famine and death and desolation in their wake.

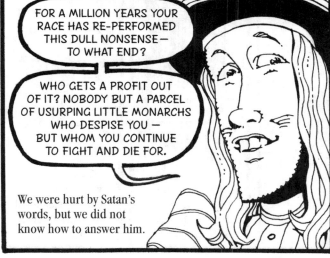

FOR A MILLION YEARS YOUR RACE HAS RE-PERFORMED THIS DULL NONSENSE— TO WHAT END?

WHO GETS A PROFIT OUT OF IT? NOBODY BUT A PARCEL OF USURPING LITTLE MONARCHS WHO DESPISE YOU — BUT WHOM YOU CONTINUE TO FIGHT AND DIE FOR.

We were hurt by Satan's words, but we did not know how to answer him.

Poor Seppi looked distressed, and I was deeply depressed.

Meanwhile, our people were witch-hunting. They caught a lady who was known to have the habit of curing people by devilish arts, such as bathing and nourishing them instead of bleeding them in the proper way.

They dragged her to a tree to be hanged.

As she passed me, I threw a stone, although in my heart I was sorry for her.

But all were throwing stones and if I had not done as the others did, it would have been noticed.

Satan burst out laughing.

IN FEAR, YOU STONED THE WOMAN WHEN YOUR HEART REVOLTED AT THE ACT. OH, BUT YOUR RACE IS MADE UP OF SHEEP!

GOVERNMENTS, ARISTOCRACIES, AND RELIGIONS ARE ALL BASED UPON THAT LARGE DEFECT IN YOUR RACE— MAN'S DISTRUST OF HIS NEIGHBOR, AND HIS DESIRE TO STAND WELL IN HIS NEIGHBOR'S EYE.

With that, Satan vanished. The following days were dull without him.

At last, Father Peter's trial came, and people gathered from all around to witness it. Marget asked Wilhelm Meidling to defend her uncle.

If Satan would only come! Of course I did not doubt that the case would be won, and that Father Peter would be happy for the rest of his life, since Satan had said so.

Everybody was there except the accused. He was too feeble for the strain.

The money was emptied on a table, and was examined by such as were privileged.

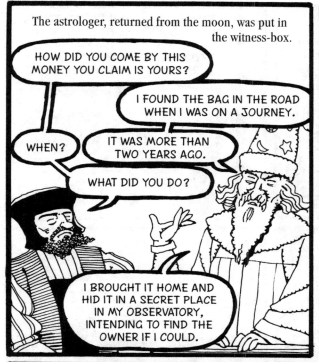

The astrologer, returned from the moon, was put in the witness-box.

HOW DID YOU COME BY THIS MONEY YOU CLAIM IS YOURS?

I FOUND THE BAG IN THE ROAD WHEN I WAS ON A JOURNEY.

WHEN?

IT WAS MORE THAN TWO YEARS AGO.

WHAT DID YOU DO?

I BROUGHT IT HOME AND HID IT IN A SECRET PLACE IN MY OBSERVATORY, INTENDING TO FIND THE OWNER IF I COULD.

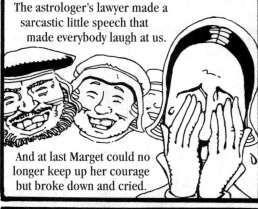

SOME TIME LATER, I TOOK IT OUT AND COUNTED IT. AND THEN... I AM SORRY TO HAVE TO SAY THIS, BUT JUST AS I HAD FINISHED, I LOOKED UP AND THERE STOOD FATHER PETER BEHIND ME.

AFTER I HEARD OF FATHER PETER'S FIND I CAME HOME AND DISCOVERED THAT MY OWN MONEY WAS GONE. HE HAD FOUND EXACTLY THE SAME SUM AS I HAD LOST.

Wilhelm Meidling then called us boys, and we told our tale.

It might be difficult for people to believe the astrologer's story, considering his character, but it was almost impossible to believe ours.

The astrologer's lawyer made a sarcastic little speech that made everybody laugh at us.

And at last Marget could no longer keep up her courage but broke down and cried.

Then I saw something that braced me up. Satan was standing alongside of Wilhelm! No one else noticed Satan, so I knew that he was invisible.

Satan then began to melt into Wilhelm, and his spirit looked out of the lawyer's eyes.

He then confronted the accuser.

YOU HAVE TESTIFIED THAT YOU FOUND THIS MONEY MORE THAN TWO YEARS AGO.

THAT IS CORRECT.

AND THE MONEY WAS NEVER OUT OF YOUR HANDS UP TO THE LAST DAY OF LAST YEAR?

ALSO CORRECT.

IF I PROVE THE MONEY HERE IS NOT THAT HE FOUND, THEN IT IS NOT HIS?

CERTAINLY NOT; BUT IF YOU HAVE A NEW WITNESS YOU MUST GIVE PROPER NOTICE.

BUT I SPEAK OF THE COIN ITSELF. IT WAS NOT IN EXISTENCE LAST DECEMBER. OBSERVE THE DATES.

ALL OF THE COINS ARE OF THIS PRESENT YEAR. THE COURT TENDERS ITS SINCERE SYMPATHY TO THE ACCUSED. THE CASE IS DISMISSED!

Everybody rushed forward to congratulate Marget and Wilhelm.

Satan was gone. I judged that he had spirited himself away to the jail.

But Satan had told Father Peter that he stood disgraced as a thief — by verdict of the court!

The shock of this unseated the old priest's reason.

When we arrived, he was parading around and delivering commands. He thought he was the Emperor!

IT IS NOT BECOMING FOR THE CROWN PRINCESS TO CRY. JUST TELL ME YOUR TROUBLE AND IT SHALL BE MENDED!

Marget and Ursula walked him home, crying all the way. It was as pitiful a sight as ever I saw. I reproached Satan for deceiving me.

IT WAS THE TRUTH. I SAID HE WOULD BE HAPPY, AND HE IS NOW THE ONE UTTERLY HAPPY PERSON IN THIS EMPIRE.

NO SANE MAN CAN BE HAPPY. IT SEEMS TO ME THAT YOU ARE HARD TO PLEASE.

For a year Satan continued his visits, but then he came less often. When one day he finally visited, I was overjoyed.

OUR TIME TOGETHER HAS BEEN PLEASANT, BUT WE SHALL NOT SEE EACH OTHER ANY MORE.

BUT SURELY WE SHALL MEET IN ANOTHER LIFE, SATAN.

NO, THERE IS NO OTHER LIFE. IT IS NOT REAL!

So the afterlife is only a vision… a dream! I had held that very thought a thousand times!

GOD — MAN — THE WORLD — THE STARS ARE ALL A DREAM. AND I MYSELF AM BUT A CREATURE OF YOUR IMAGINATION!

STRANGE THAT YOU SHOULD NOT HAVE SUSPECTED AGES AGO, FOR YOUR UNIVERSE AND ITS CONTENTS ARE SO FRANKLY AND HYSTERICALLY INSANE.

A GOD WHO COULD MAKE EVERY PERSON HAPPY, YET GIVES THEM MISERIES AND MALADIES; WHO MOUTHS MERCY AND INVENTED HELL; WHO CREATED MAN WITHOUT INVITATION, THEN TRIES TO SHUFFLE THE RESPONSIBILITY FOR MAN'S ACTS UPON MAN; AND FINALLY REQUIRES THIS POOR, ABUSED SLAVE TO WORSHIP HIM! THESE THINGS ARE IMPOSSIBLE EXCEPT IN A HORRIBLE DREAM!

AND NOTHING EXISTS BUT YOU, A VAGRANT THOUGHT, WANDERING AMONG THE EMPTY ETERNITIES!

He vanished, and left me appalled; for I realized that all he had said was true.

Ende

WRITTEN BY MARK TWAIN

HOW The AUTHOR WAS SOLD in NEWARK

ADAPTED BY MILTON KNIGHT.

YOU MAY REMEMBER THAT I LECTURED IN NEWARK LATELY?

DURING THE AFTERNOON, I TALKED WITH A YOUNG MAN WHO HAD ATTENDED MY LECTURE.

HE SAID HE HAD AN UNCLE WHO, FROM SOME CAUSE OR OTHER, SEEMED TO HAVE GROWN PERMANENTLY BEREFT OF ALL EMOTION.

OH, IF I COULD ONLY SEE HIM *LAUGH* ONCE MORE!--

IF I COULD ONLY SEE HIM

I NEVER COULD WITHSTAND DISTRESS.

MY SON, BRING THE OLD PARTY ROUND. I HAVE SOME JOKES THAT WILL MAKE HIM LAUGH, CRY... OR KILL HIM.

THE YOUNG MAN PLACED HIS UNCLE IN FULL VIEW THAT NIGHT---

AND I BEGAN ON HIM.

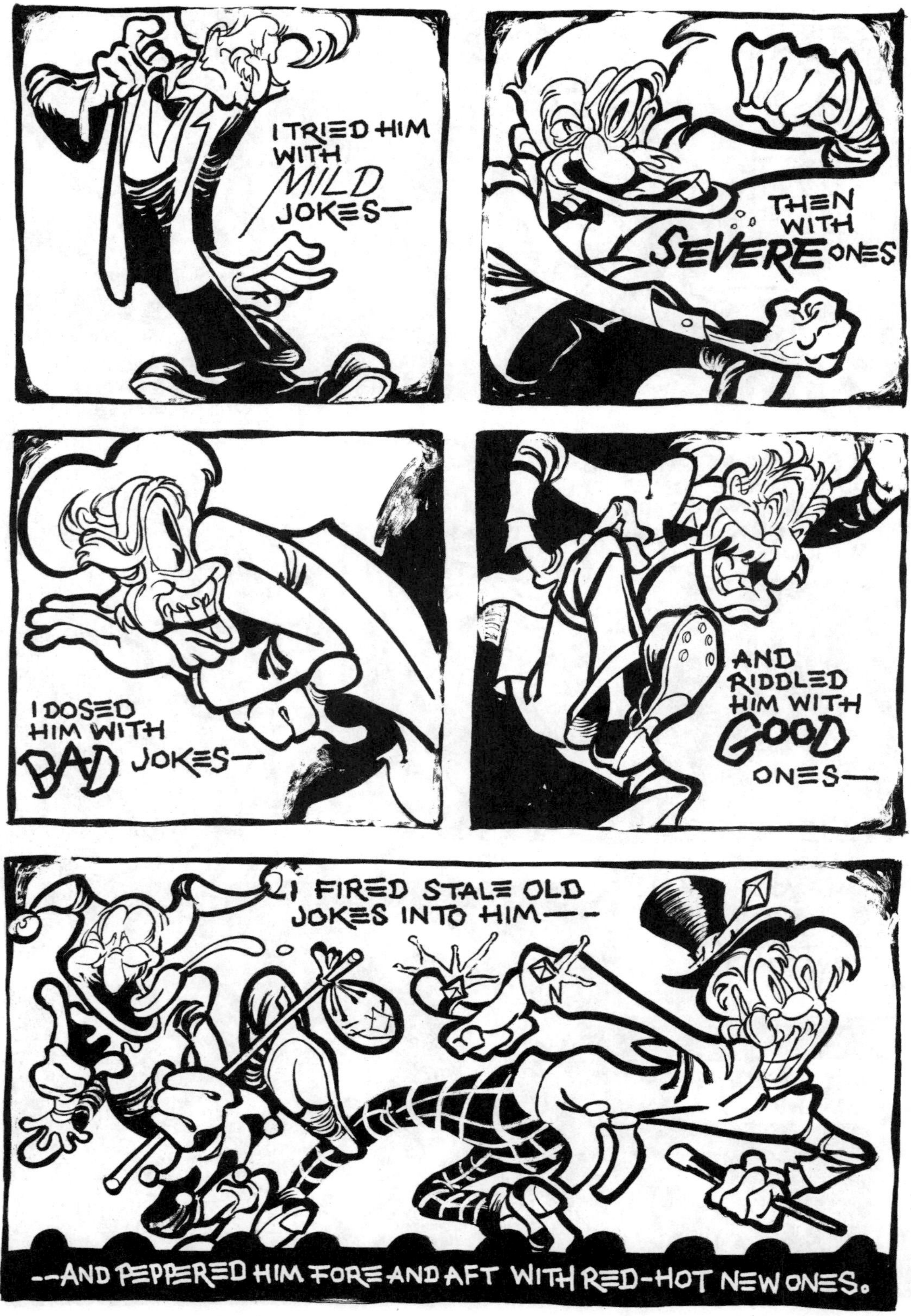
I TRIED HIM WITH MILD JOKES—
THEN WITH SEVERE ONES
I DOSED HIM WITH BAD JOKES—
AND RIDDLED HIM WITH GOOD ONES—
I FIRED STALE OLD JOKES INTO HIM---
--AND PEPPERED HIM FORE AND AFT WITH RED-HOT NEW ONES.

I WARMED UP TO MY WORK AND ASSAULTED HIM *RIGHT* AND *LEFT*, IN *FRONT* AND *BEHIND*

'FUMED AND SWEATED AND CHARGED AND RANTED 'TIL I WAS HOARSE AND SICK AND FRANTIC AND FURIOUS

BUT I NEVER MOVED HIM ONCE --- NEVER A GHOST OF A SMILE — NEVER A SUSPICION OF MOISTURE!

I CLOSED THE LECTURE WITH *ONE DESPAIRING SHRIEK*

—AND HURLED A JOKE OF *SUPERNATURAL* ATROCITY *FULL AT HIM!*

THE PRESIDENT OF THE SOCIETY ASKED:

WHAT MADE YOU CARRY ON SO TOWARD THE LAST?

I WAS *TRYING TO MAKE* THAT CONFOUNDED OLD FOOL LAUGH.

WELL, YOU WERE WASTING YOUR TIME, BECAUSE HE IS *DEAF, DUMB* AND AS *BLIND* AS A BADGER!

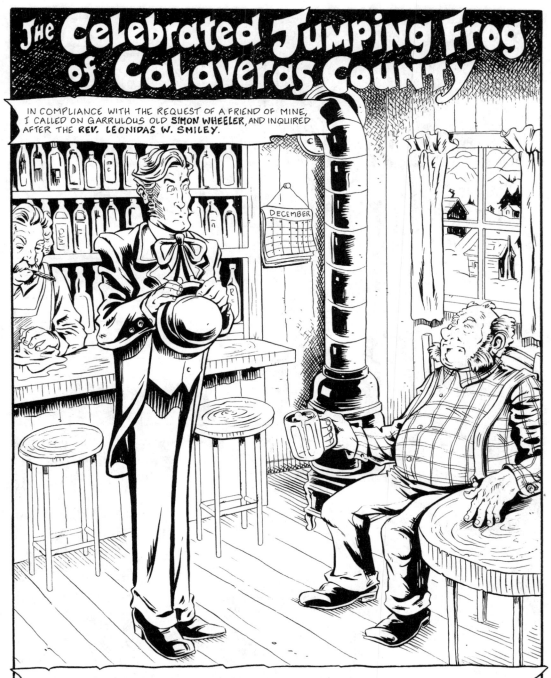

The Celebrated Jumping Frog of Calaveras County

IN COMPLIANCE WITH THE REQUEST OF A FRIEND OF MINE, I CALLED ON GARRULOUS OLD **SIMON WHEELER**, AND INQUIRED AFTER THE **REV. LEONIDAS W. SMILEY.**

I FOUND SIMON WHEELER DOZING COMFORTABLY BY THE BAR-ROOM STOVE OF THE DILAPIDATED TAVERN IN THE ANCIENT MINING CAMP OF ANGEL'S. HE ROUSED UP AND GAVE ME A GOOD DAY. I TOLD HIM A FRIEND OF MINE HAD COMMISSIONED ME TO MAKE SOME INQUIRIES ABOUT A COMPANION OF HIS BOYHOOD NAMED LEONIDAS W. SMILEY- A YOUNG MINISTER OF THE GOSPEL, WHO HE HAD HEARD WAS A RESIDENT OF ANGEL'S CAMP.

ADAPTED & ILLUSTRATED BY KEVIN ATKINSON

SIMON WHEELER BACKED ME INTO A CORNER AND BLOCKADED ME THERE WITH HIS CHAIR, AND THEN SAT ME DOWN AND REELED OFF THE FOLLOWING NARRATIVE:

THERE WAS A FELLER HERE ONCE BY THE NAME OF **JIM SMILEY**, IN THE WINTER OF '49...

"...OR MAYBE IT WAS THE SPRING OF '50 — I DON'T RECALL EXACTLY, BUT ANY WAY, HE WAS THE CURIOUSEST MAN ABOUT ALWAYS BETTING ON ANYTHING YOU EVER SEE, IF HE COULD GET ANY BODY TO BET ON THE OTHER SIDE. AND IF HE COULDN'T, HE'D CHANGE SIDES. ANY WAY THAT SUITED THE OTHER MAN WOULD SUIT HIM."

"BUT STILL, HE WAS UNCOMMON LUCKY; HE MOST ALWAYS COME OUT A WINNER."

"JUST SO HE GOT A BET, HE WAS SATISFIED."

"THERE COULDN'T BE NO SOLITRY THING MENTIONED BUT THAT FELLER'D OFFER TO BET ON IT."

48

"IF THERE WAS A HORSE RACE, YOU'D FIND HIM FLUSH..."

"...OR YOU'D FIND HIM BUSTED AT THE END OF IT."

"IF THERE WAS A CAT FIGHT, HE'D BET ON IT."

"IF THERE WAS A CHICKEN FIGHT, HE'D BET ON IT."

"WHY, IF THERE WAS TWO BIRDS SETTIN' ON A FENCE HE WOULD BET YOU WHICH ONE WOULD FLY FIRST."

"PARSON WALKER'S WIFE LAY SICK ONCE, AND IT SEEMED AS IF THEY WARN'T GOING TO SAVE HER; BUT ONE MORNING HE COME IN, AND SMILEY ASKED HOW SHE WAS, AND HE SAID SHE WAS CONSIDERABLE BETTER AND WITH THE BLESSING OF PROV'DENCE SHE'D GET WELL YET; AND SMILEY, BEFORE HE THOUGHT SAYS."

WELL, I'LL RISK TWO-AND-A-HALF SHE **DON'T**, ANY WAY.

"THISH-YER SMILEY HAD A MARE— THE BOYS CALLED HER THE FIFTEEN-MINUTE NAG, BUT THAT WAS ONLY IN FUN, BECAUSE, OF COURSE, SHE WAS FASTER THAN THAT— AND HE USED TO WIN MONEY ON THAT HORSE, FOR ALL SHE WAS SO SLOW AND ALWAYS HAD THE ASTHMA, OR THE DISTEMPER, OR THE CONSUMPTION OR SOMETHING OF THAT KIND."

"THEY USED TO GIVE HER THREE HUNDRED YARDS START, AND THEN PASS HER UNDER WAY; BUT ALWAYS AT THE FAG-END OF THE RACE SHE'D GET EXCITED, AND COME CAVORTING UP, AND KICKING UP M-O-R-E DUST AND RAISING M-O-R-E RACKET WITH HER COUGHING AND SNEEZING AND BLOWING HER NOSE-AND ALWAYS FETCH UP AT THE STAND JUST ABOUT A NECK AHEAD."

"AND HE HAD A LITTLE BULL PUP, THAT TO LOOK AT HIM YOU'D THINK HE WAN'T WORTH A CENT, BUT TO SET AROUND AND LOOK ORNERY."

" BUT AS SOON AS MONEY WAS UP ON HIM, HE WAS A DIFFERENT DOG; HIS TEETH WOULD UNCOVER, AND SHINE SAVAGE."

"AND A DOG MIGHT TACKLE HIM, AND BITE HIM, AND THROW HIM OVER HIS SHOULDER TWO OR THREE TIMES, AND ANDREW JACKSON—WHICH WAS THE NAME OF THE PUP— ANDREW JACKSON WOULD NEVER LET ON BUT WHAT HE WAS SATISFIED, AND HADN'T EXPECTED NOTHING ELSE— AND THE BETS BEING DOUBLED ON THE OTHER SIDE ALL THE TIME, TILL THE MONEY WAS ALL UP; AND THEN ALL OF THE SUDDEN HE WOULD GRAB THAT OTHER DOG BY THE J'INT OF HIS HIND LEG AND JEST HANG ON TILL THEY THROWED UP THE SPONGE, IF IT WAS A YEAR. "

"HE GAVE SMILEY A LOOK, AS MUCH TO SAY HIS HEART WAS BROKE, AND IT WAS HIS FAULT FOR PUTTING UP A DOG THAT HADN'T NO LEGS FOR HIM TO TAKE HOLT OF WHICH WAS HIS MAIN DEPENDENCE IN A FIGHT. "

"SMILEY ALWAYS COME OUT A WINNER ON THAT PUP, TILL HE HARNESSED A DOG ONCE THAT DIDN'T HAVE NO HIND LEGS, BECAUSE THEY'D BEEN SAWED OFF BY A CIRCULAR SAW, AND WHEN THE THING HAD GONE FAR ENOUGH AND THE MONEY WAS ALL UP, AND HE COME TO MAKE A SNATCH FOR HIS PET HOLT, HE SAW IN A MINUTE HOW HE'D BEEN IMPOSED ON, AND HE DIDN'T TRY NO MORE TO WIN THE FIGHT, AND SO HE GOT SHUCKED OUT BAD."

"AND THEN HE LIMPED OFF A PIECE AND LAYED DOWN AND DIED. "

"IT WAS A GOOD PUP, THAT ANDREW JACKSON. IT ALWAYS MAKES ME FEEL SORRY WHEN I THINK OF THAT LAST FIGHT OF HIS'N AND THE WAY IT TURNED OUT. "

"WELL, THISH-YER SMILEY HAD RAT-TARRIERS, AND CHICKEN COCKS, AND TOM-CATS, AND ALL THEM KIND OF THINGS, AND YOU COULDN'T FETCH NOTHING FOR HIM TO BET ON BUT HE'D MATCH YOU."

"HE KETCHED A FROG ONE DAY, AND TOOK HIM HOME, AND SAID HE CAL'KLATED TO EDERCATE HIM."

"AND SO HE NEVER DONE NOTHING FOR THREE MONTHS BUT SET IN HIS BACK YARD AND LEARN THAT FROG TO JUMP."

"AND YOU BET HE DID LEARN HIM, TOO. HE'D GIVE HIM A LITTLE PUNCH BEHIND, AND THE NEXT MINUTE YOU'D SEE HIM WHIRLING IN THE AIR AND COME DOWN FLAT-FOOTED LIKE A CAT. DAN'L WEBSTER WAS THE NAME OF THE FROG, AND WHEN IT COME TO JUMP-ING ON A LEVEL, HE COULD GET OVER MORE GROUND AT ONE STRADDLE THAN ANY ANIMAL OF HIS BREED YOU EVER SEE."

"SMILEY WAS MONSTROUS PROUD OF HIS FROG, AS WELL HE MIGHT BE, FOR FELLERS THAT HAD TRAVELED AND BEEN EVERYWHERES, ALL SAID HE LAID OVER ANY FROG THEY EVER SEE."

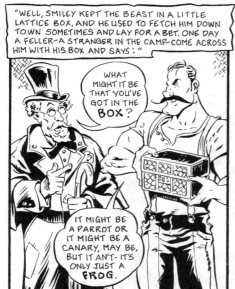

"WELL, SMILEY KEPT THE BEAST IN A LITTLE LATTICE BOX, AND HE USED TO FETCH HIM DOWN TOWN SOMETIMES AND LAY FOR A BET. ONE DAY A FELLER—A STRANGER IN THE CAMP—COME ACROSS HIM WITH HIS BOX AND SAYS:"

WHAT MIGHT IT BE THAT YOU'VE GOT IN THE BOX?

IT MIGHT BE A PARROT OR IT MIGHT BE A CANARY, MAY BE, BUT IT AN'T—IT'S ONLY JUST A FROG.

"AND THE FELLER LOOKED AT IT CAREFUL AND SAYS..."

H'M—SO 'TIS.. WELL, WHAT'S HE GOOD FOR?

HE'S GOOD FOR ONE THING...

...HE CAN OUT JUMP ANY FROG IN CALAVERAS COUNTY.

"THE FELLER TOOK THE BOX AGAIN, AND TOOK ANOTHER LONG, PARTICULAR LOOK, AND GIVE IT BACK TO SMILEY AND SAYS VERY DELIBERATE..."

WELL, I DON'T SEE NO P'NTS ABOUT THAT FROG THAT'S ANY BETTER 'N' ANY OTHER FROG.

MAY BE YOU DON'T. MAY BE YOU UNDERSTAND FROGS, AND MAY BE YOU DON'T UNDERSTAND 'EM.

ANYWAYS I'VE GOT MY OPINION AND I'LL RISK FORTY DOLLARS THAT SAYS HE CAN OUTJUMP ANY FROG IN CALAVERAS COUNTY.

"THEN THE FELLER SAYS, KINDA SAD LIKE..."

WELL, I'M ONLY A STRANGER HERE, AND I AN'T GOT NO FROG; BUT IF I HAD A FROG, I'D BET YOU.

THAT'S ALL RIGHT— THAT'S ALL RIGHT—IF YOU HOLD MY BOX A MINUTE, I'LL GO GET YOU A FROG.

"AND SO THE FELLER TOOK THE BOX AND SET DOWN TO WAIT."

"HE SAT THERE A GOOD WHILE THINKING TO HISSELF, AND THEN HE GOT THE FROG OUT AND PRIZED HIS MOUTH OPEN AND TOOK A TEASPOON AND FILLED HIM FULL OF QUAIL SHOT- FILLED HIM PRETTY NEAR UP TO HIS CHIN..."

"...AND SET HIM ON THE FLOOR."

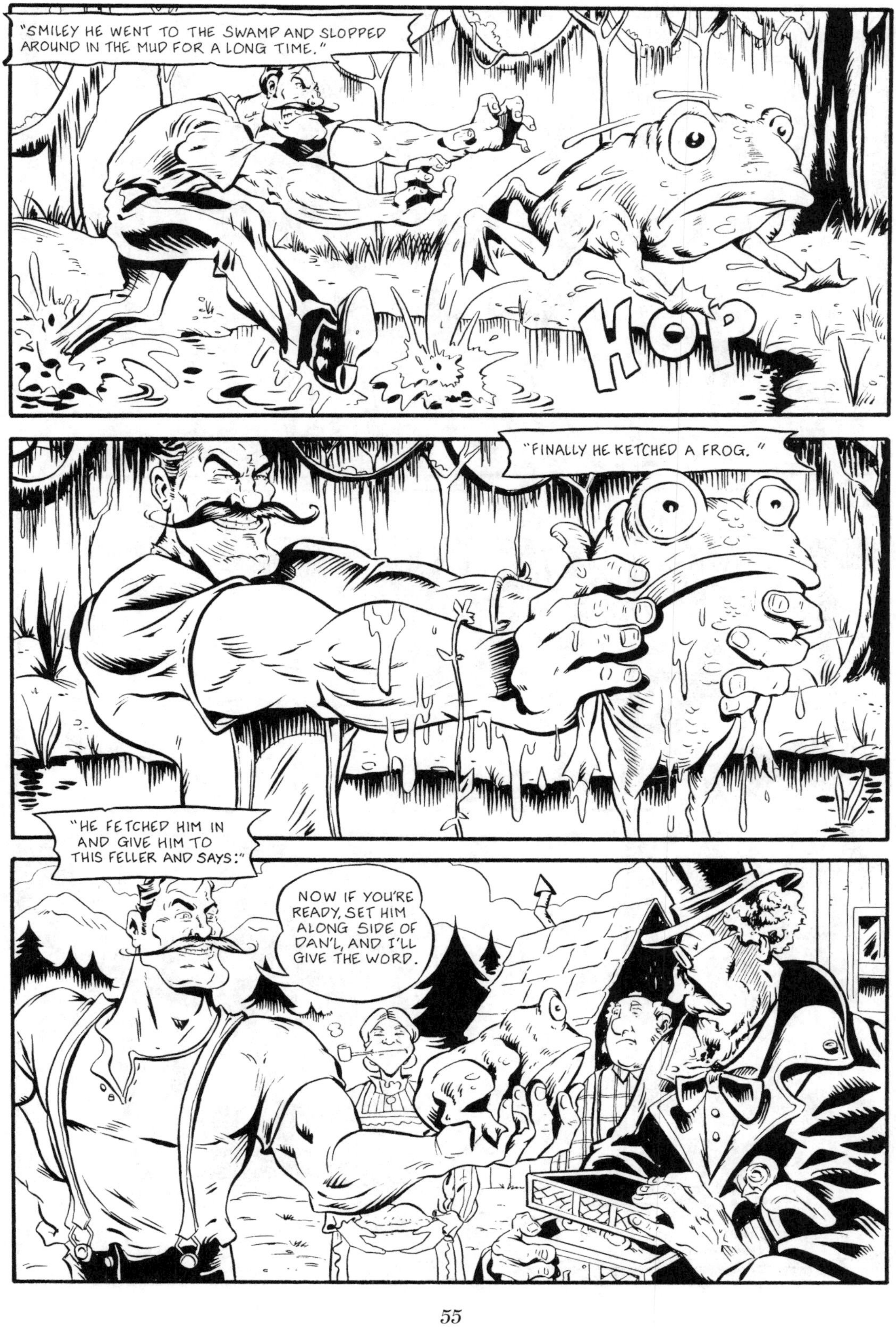
"SMILEY HE WENT TO THE SWAMP AND SLOPPED AROUND IN THE MUD FOR A LONG TIME."
HOP
"FINALLY HE KETCHED A FROG."
"HE FETCHED HIM IN AND GIVE HIM TO THIS FELLER AND SAYS:"
NOW IF YOU'RE READY, SET HIM ALONG SIDE OF DAN'L, AND I'LL GIVE THE WORD.

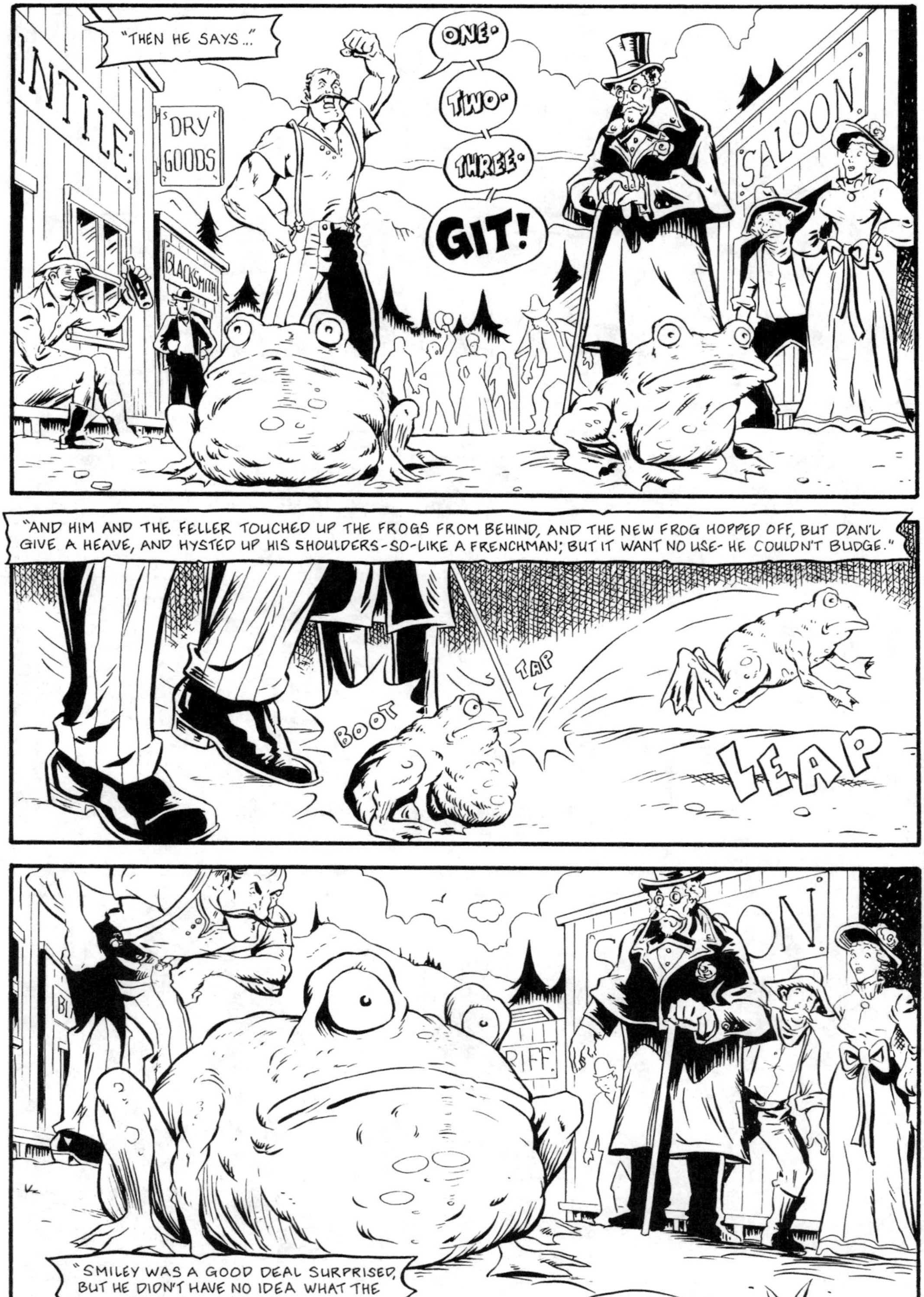
"THEN HE SAYS..."
ONE-
TWO-
THREE-
GIT!
INTILE
DRY GOODS
BLACKSMITH
SALOON
"AND HIM AND THE FELLER TOUCHED UP THE FROGS FROM BEHIND, AND THE NEW FROG HOPPED OFF, BUT DAN'L GIVE A HEAVE, AND HYSTED UP HIS SHOULDERS-SO-LIKE A FRENCHMAN; BUT IT WANT NO USE- HE COULDN'T BUDGE."
TAP
BOOT
LEAP
RIFF.
"SMILEY WAS A GOOD DEAL SURPRISED, BUT HE DIDN'T HAVE NO IDEA WHAT THE MATTER WAS, OF COURSE."

"THE FELLER TOOK THE MONEY AND STARTED AWAY, AND SORTA JERKED HIS THUMB AT DAN'L AND SAYS..."

WELL, I DON'T SEE NO P'INTS ABOUT THAT FROG THAT'S ANY BETTER'N ANY OTHER FROG.

"SMILEY SCRATCHES HIS HEAD AND LOOKING DOWN AT DAN'L SAYS..."

I WONDER IF THERE AN'T SOMETHIN THE MATTER WITH THIS FROG?

HE 'PEARS TO LOOK MIGHTY BAGGY, SOMEHOW.

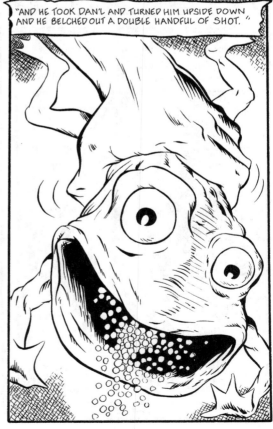

"AND HE TOOK DAN'L AND TURNED HIM UPSIDE DOWN AND HE BELCHED OUT A DOUBLE HANDFUL OF SHOT."

"AND THEN HE SEE HOW IT WAS ..."

"HE TOOK OUT AFTER THAT FELLER, BUT HE NEVER KETCHED HIM. AND —"

BUT I DID NOT THINK THAT A CONTINUATION OF THE HISTORY OF JIM SMILEY WOULD BE LIKELY TO AFFORD ME MUCH INFORMATION CONCERNING THE REV. LEONIDAS W. SMILEY, AND SO I STARTED AWAY.

WELL, THISH-YER SMILEY HAD A YALLER ONE-EYED COW THAT DIDN'T HAVE NO TAIL, ONLY JEST A SHORT STUMP LIKE A BANNANNER, AND—

"OH, HANG SMILEY AND HIS AFFLICTED COW!" I MUTTERED AND BIDDING THE OLD GENTLEMAN A GOOD DAY, I DEPARTED.

The Legend of Sagenfeld

*M*ORE THAN A THOUSAND YEARS AGO there was a kingdom far removed from the turmoils of that old warlike day. In the course of time the old king died and his little son Hubert came to the throne. Now at his birth the soothsayers had diligently studied the stars and found something written in that shining book to this effect:

In Hubert's fourteenth year, a pregnant event will happen; the animal whose singing shall sound sweetest in Hubert's ear shall save his life. So long as the king and the nation shall honor this animal's race for this good deed, the ancient dynasty shall not fail of an heir, nor the nation know war or pestilence or poverty. But beware an erring choice!

All through the king's thirteenth year but one thing was talked of by the people: How is the last sentence of the prophecy to be understood? What goes before seems to mean that the saving animal will choose itself at the proper time; but the closing sentence seems to mean that the king must choose beforehand, and say what singer among the animals pleases him best.

STORY BY **MARK TWAIN**, EDITED BY TOM POMPLUN, ILLUSTRATED BY **EVERT GERADTS**

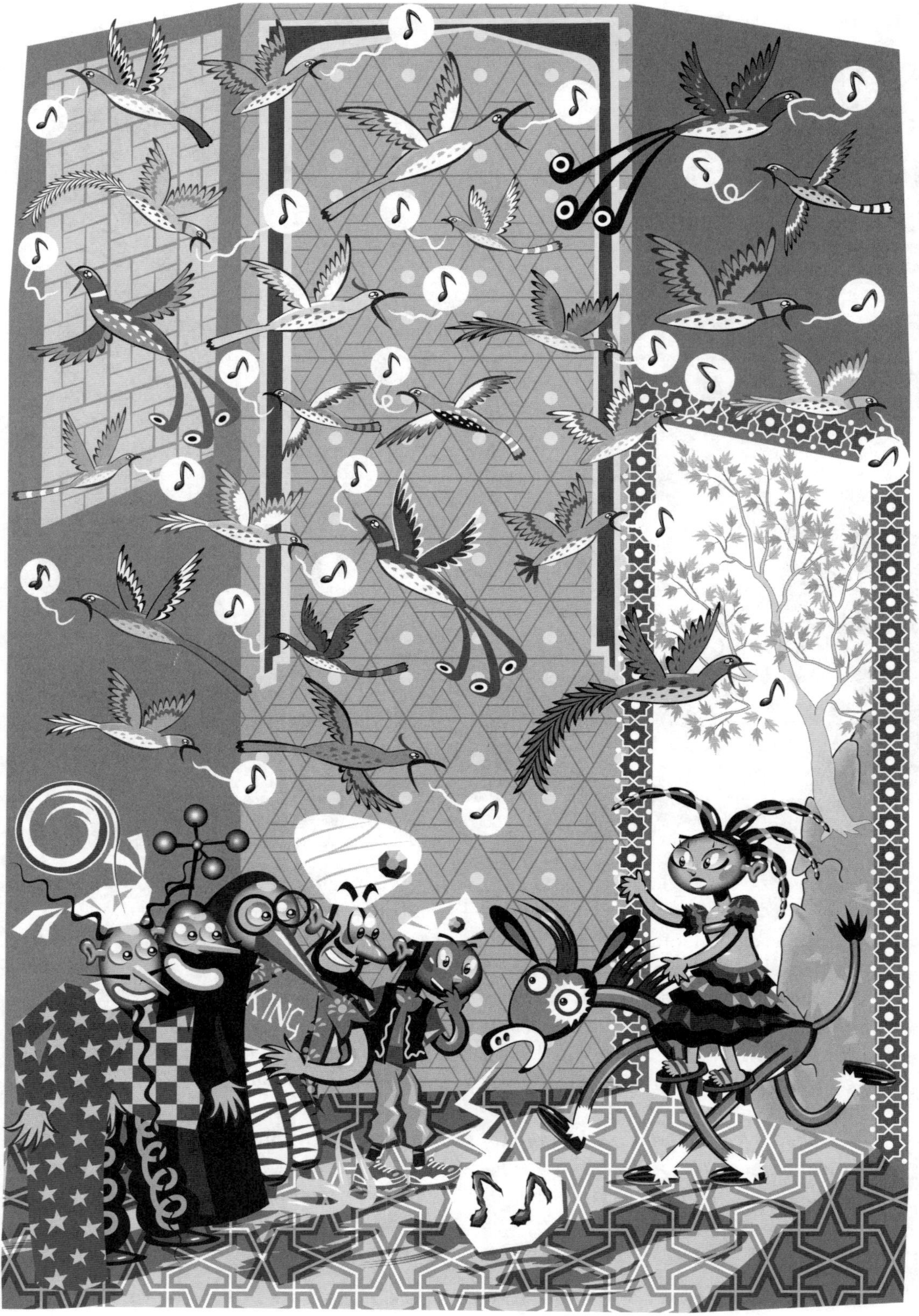
KING

There were many opinions about this matter, but a majority were agreed that the safest plan would be for the little king to make a choice beforehand, and the earlier the better. So an edict was sent forth commanding all persons who owned singing creatures to bring them to the great hall of the palace on the first day of the new year. When everything was in readiness for the trial, the king mounted his golden throne and prepared to give judgment.

One sweet warbler after another charmed the young king's ear. Among so many bewitching songsters he found it hard to choose, and all the harder because the promised penalty for an error was so terrible that it made him afraid to trust his own ears. His ministers saw this, and they began to say in their hearts:

"He has lost courage — he will err — he and his people are doomed!"

At the end of an hour the king sat silent awhile, and then said:

"Bring back the linnet."

The linnet trilled forth her jubilant music. In the midst of it the king was about to uplift his scepter in sign of choice, but checked himself and said:

"But let us be sure. Bring back the thrush; let them sing together."

The thrush was brought, and the two birds poured out their song together. The king wavered, then his inclination began to strengthen. Hope budded in the hearts of the old ministers, when there was a hideous sound at the door:

"Waw...he! waw-he! waw-he! waw-he!"

Everybody was startled when a little peasant-maid of nine years came tripping in, her eyes glowing with childish eagerness; but when she saw that august company and those angry faces she stopped and hung her head. Presently she looked up timidly through her tears, and she said:

"My lord the king, I pray you pardon me, for I meant no wrong. I have no father and no mother, but I have a goat and a donkey, and they are all in all to me. My goat gives me the sweetest milk, and when my donkey brays it seems to me there is no music like to it. So when the king's jester said the sweetest singer among all the animals should save the crown and nation, it moved me to bring him here —"

All the court burst into a rude laugh, and the child fled away crying. The chief minister gave an order that she and her donkey be flogged beyond the precincts of the palace and commanded to come within them no more.

Then the trial of the birds was resumed. An hour went by; two hours; still no decision. The day waned to its close, and the waiting multitudes outside the palace grew crazed with anxiety. The great trial had failed; and all wished to hide the trouble in their hearts.

Finally, a rich, full strain of the divinest melody streamed forth from a remote part of the hall. It was the nightingale's voice!

"Up!" shouted the king, "let all the bells make proclamation to the people, for the choice is made and we have not erred. King, dynasty, and nation are saved. From henceforth let the nightingale be honored throughout the land forever. And publish it among all the people that whosoever shall insult a nightingale, or injure it, shall suffer death. The king hath spoken."

The people danced and drank and sang; and the triumphant clamor of the bells never ceased.

From that day the nightingale was a sacred bird. Its song was heard in every house. The poets wrote its praises, the painters painted it, and its sculptured image adorned every public building.

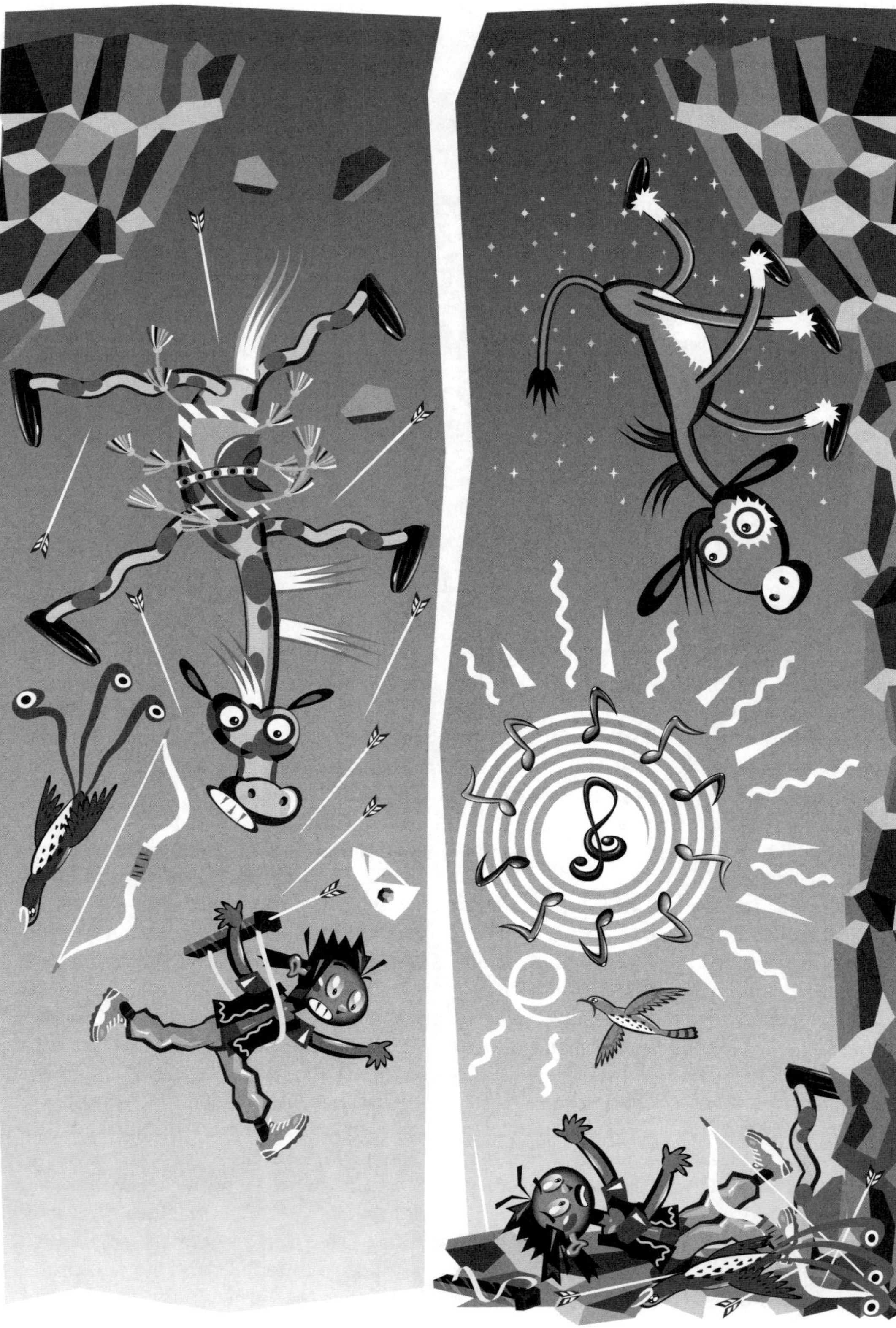

THE YOUNG KING was very fond of the chase. When the summer was come he rode forth with hawk and hound one day in a company of his nobles. He got separated from them in a great forest, and rode on and on, with sinking courage. Twilight came on, and then came a catastrophe. In the dim light he forced his horse through a tangled thicket overhanging a steep declivity. When horse and rider reached the bottom, the former had a broken neck and the latter a broken leg. The king lay there suffering agonies of pain, and each hour seemed a month to him. At last he gave up all hope, and said, "Let death come, for come it must."

Just then the deep, sweet song of a nightingale swept across the still wastes of the night.

"Saved!" the king said. "It is the sacred bird, and the prophecy is come true! The gods themselves protected me from error in the choice."

He could hardly contain his joy. Every few moments, he thought he caught the sound of approaching succor. But each time it was a disappointment; the dull hours drifted on. Still no help came — but still the sacred bird sang on. The king began to have misgivings about his choice. The morning came, and with it thirst and hunger. The day waxed and waned. At last the king cursed the nightingale.

Then he lay many hours insensible. When he came to himself, the dawn of the third morning was breaking. Ah, the world seemed very beautiful to those worn eyes. Suddenly a great longing to live rose up in the lad's heart, and from his soul welled a deep and fervent prayer that Heaven would have mercy upon him and let him see his home and his friends once more. In that instant a faint sound, but oh, how inexpressibly sweet to his waiting ear, came floating out of the distance:

"Waw ... he! waw-he! waw-he! waw-he!"

"Oh, that song is a thousand times sweeter than the voice of the nightingale, for indeed, am I saved! The sacred singer has chosen itself, and the prophecy is fulfilled."

Down the declivity the little donkey wandered, cropping herbage as he went; and when at last he saw the dead horse and the wounded king, he came and snuffed at them with curiosity. The king petted him, and with great labor and pain, drew himself upon the creature's back. The ass carried the king to the little peasant-maid's hut. She gave him her bed, refreshed him with goat's milk, and then flew to tell the news to the searchers.

The king got well. His first act was to proclaim the sacredness and inviolability of the ass; his second was to add this particular ass to his cabinet and make him chief minister of the crown; his third was to have all the statues of nightingales throughout his kingdom destroyed, and replaced by statues of the sacred donkey; and, his fourth was to announce that when the little peasant-maid should reach her fifteenth year he would make her his queen.

Such is the legend. And this explains why the moldering image of the ass adorns all these old crumbling walls and arches; and it explains why, during many centuries, an ass was always the chief minister in that royal cabinet, just as is still the case in most cabinets to this day; and it also explains why, in that little kingdom, during many centuries, all great poems, all great speeches, all great books, all public solemnities, and all royal proclamations always began with these stirring words:

"Waw ... he! waw-he! waw-he! waw-he!"

Ode to Stephen Dowling Bots, Dec'd.

an excerpt from The Adventures of Huckleberry Finn
by **Mark Twain**
illustrated by **Jackie Smith**

And did young Stephen sicken,
And did young Stephen die?
And did the sad hearts thicken,
And did the mourners cry?

No; such was not the fate of
Young Stephen Dowling Bots;
Though sad hearts round him thickened,
'Twas not from sickness' shots.

No whooping-cough did rack his frame,
Nor measles drear, with spots;
Not these impaired the sacred name
Of Stephen Dowling Bots.

Despised love struck not with woe
That head of curly knots,
Nor stomach troubles laid him low,
Young Stephen Dowling Bots.

O no. Then list with tearful eye,
Whilst I his fate do tell.
His soul did from this cold world fly,
By falling down a well.

They got him out and emptied him;
Alas it was too late;
His spirit was gone for to sport aloft
In the realms of the good and great.

ILLUSTRATIONS ©2004 JACKIE SMITH

Prelude:

P.T. BARNUM and the CARDIFF GIANT

by **Tom Pomplun**
illustrated by **Dan E. Burr**

There were giants in the earth in those days; and also after that, when the sons of God came unto the daughters of men, and they bore children to them...

- Genesis 6:4

TEN FEET HIGH, WITH 21-INCH FEET, WEIGHING 3000 POUNDS, A NAKED, *PETRIFIED MAN* WAS DISCOVERED IN OCTOBER, 1869 IN CARDIFF, NEW YORK, BY TWO LABORERS DIGGING A WELL ON THE FARM OF STUBB NEWELL.

LOOK! IT'S A GIANT!

HE'S BEEN TURNED TO STONE!

SCIENTISTS IMMEDIATELY BRANDED THE "FOSSIL" A *FRAUD*, CARVED FROM A SLAB OF GYPSUM, BUT THAT DID NOT DETER THE HUNDREDS OF VISITORS A DAY WHO FLOCKED TO THE FARM, PAYING TO SEE PROOF OF THE *BIBLICAL GOLIATH*.

IT WAS FORETOLD IN THE BIBLE!

IT IS A CLUMSY FAKE!

NEWELL AND TOBACCONIST *GEORGE HULL*, WHO ORIGINATED THE ENTIRE SCHEME, SOON SOLD THEIR NEW DISCOVERY TO A SYNDICATE WHICH THEN EX-HIBITED THE CARDIFF GIANT TO STILL *LARGER CROWDS* AT A MUSEUM IN SYRACUSE.

CONTRACT

THE SUCCESFUL ATTRACTION SOON DREW THE ATTENTION OF MASTER SHOWMAN *P. T. BARNUM*, WHO DESIRED TO EXHIBIT THE GIANT AS PART OF HIS TOURING CIRCUS.

THERE'S A SUCKER BORN EVERY MINUTE!

New-York Tribune

WHEN THE OWNERS REFUSED BARNUM'S OFFER, HE HAD A DUPLICATE CARDIFF GIANT CREATED, AND AS *MARK TWAIN* SAYS, "THE ORIGINAL FRAUD WAS INGENIOUSLY AND FRAUDFULLY DUPLICATED."

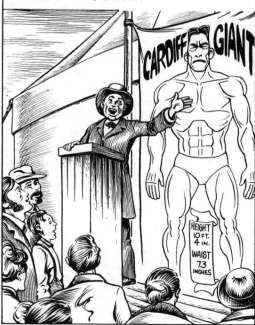

WHEN BOTH GIANTS WERE EXHIBITED IN NEW YORK CITY AT THE SAME TIME, BARNUM'S COPY DREW LARGER CROWDS THAN THE ORIGINAL, WHICH IS TODAY ON DISPLAY AT THE *FARMER'S MUSEUM* IN COOPERSTOWN, NEW YORK.

CARDIFF GIANT

HEIGHT 10 FT. 4 IN. WAIST 73 INCHES

THE CURIOUS CAN ALSO VIEW BARNUM'S CARDIFF GIANT AT *MARVIN'S MARVELOUS MECHANICAL MUSEUM* IN FARMINGTON HILLS, MICHIGAN, OR A COPY OF BARNUM'S VERSION AT THE *CIRCUS WORLD MUSEUM* IN BARABOO, WISCONSIN.

IT'S A FAKE OF A FAKE OF A FAKE!

AMAZING!

A GHOST STORY

written by Mark Twain ✦ adapted by Anton Emdin

I took a large room, far up Broadway, in a huge old building whose upper stories had been wholly unoccupied for years.

The place had long been given up to dust and cobwebs.

I seemed to be invading the privacy of the dead, that first night I climbed up to my quarters

For the first time in my life a superstitious dread came over me...

...and as I turned a dark angle of the stairway and an invisible cobweb clung to my face, I shuddered as one who had encountered a phantom

phew

I was glad when I reached my room and locked out the mould and the darkness

aaah

For two hours I sat there, thinking of bygone times, and summoning half-forgotten faces out of the mists of the past

The angry beating of the rain against the panes diminished to a tranquil patter, and one by one the noises in the street subsided, until the hurrying footsteps of the last belated straggler died away in the distance ~

The fire had burned low, and a sense of loneliness crept over me. I arose and un-dressed, then I covered up in bed, and lay listening to the rain and the faint creaking of distant shutters till they lulled me to sleep

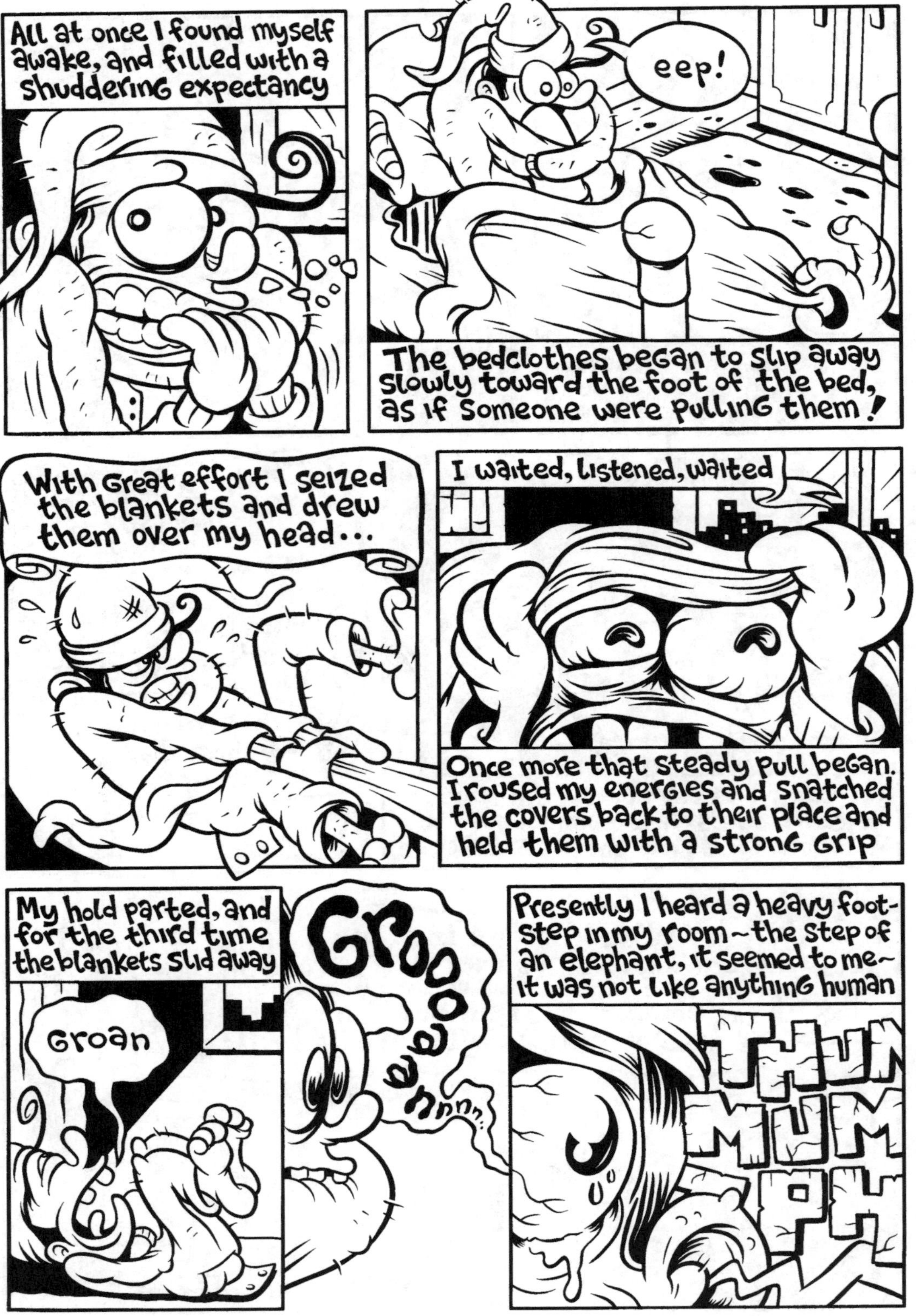
All at once I found myself awake, and filled with a shuddering expectancy
eep!
The bedclothes began to slip away slowly toward the foot of the bed, as if someone were pulling them!
With great effort I seized the blankets and drew them over my head...
I waited, listened, waited
Once more that steady pull began. I roused my energies and snatched the covers back to their place and held them with a strong grip
My hold parted, and for the third time the blankets slid away
Groan
Groooaaannnn
Presently I heard a heavy foot-step in my room ~ the step of an elephant, it seemed to me ~ it was not like anything human
THUN MUM PH

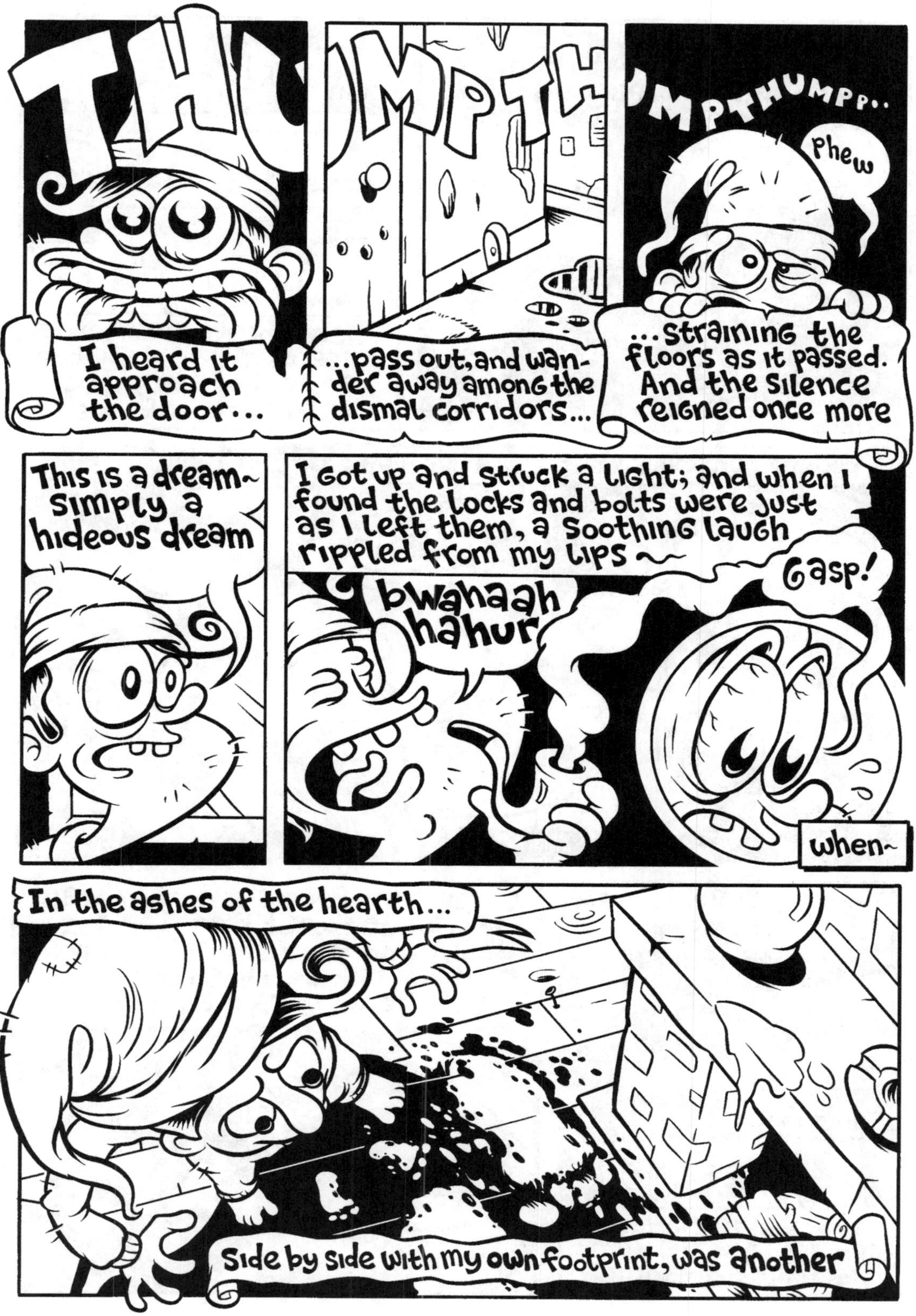
THUMPTHUMPTHUMPTHUMPP..
Phew
I heard it approach the door...
...pass out, and wander away among the dismal corridors...
...straining the floors as it passed. And the silence reigned once more
This is a dream~ simply a hideous dream
I got up and struck a light; and when I found the locks and bolts were just as I left them, a soothing laugh rippled from my lips ~~
bwahaaah hahur
Gasp!
when~
In the ashes of the hearth...
side by side with my own footprint, was another

I put out the light and returned to bed, palsied with fear. I lay a long time, peering into the darkness, and listening

Then I heard a grating noise overhead, like the dragging of a heavy body across the floor

I became conscious that I was not alone

Then the sounds ceased, and a solemn stillness followed

I crept out of bed, and lit the gas with a hand that trembled. I sat down and fell into a dreamy contemplation of that great footprint in the ashes

By and by its outlines began to waver and grow dim. I glanced up and the gas flame was slowly wilting away. In that same moment I heard that elephantine tread again...

The tread reached my very door and paused

The door did not open, and yet I felt a faint gust of air fan my cheek...

...and presently was conscious of a huge, cloudy presence before me

a pale glow stole over the thing; gradually its cloudy folds took shape~

an arm appeared...

...then legs, then a body...

...and last a great sad face looked out of the vapour

Stripped of its filmy housings the majestic **Cardiff Giant** loomed above me!

All my misery vanished~ for no harm could come with that benignant countenance

aaah

Why, is it nobody but you?

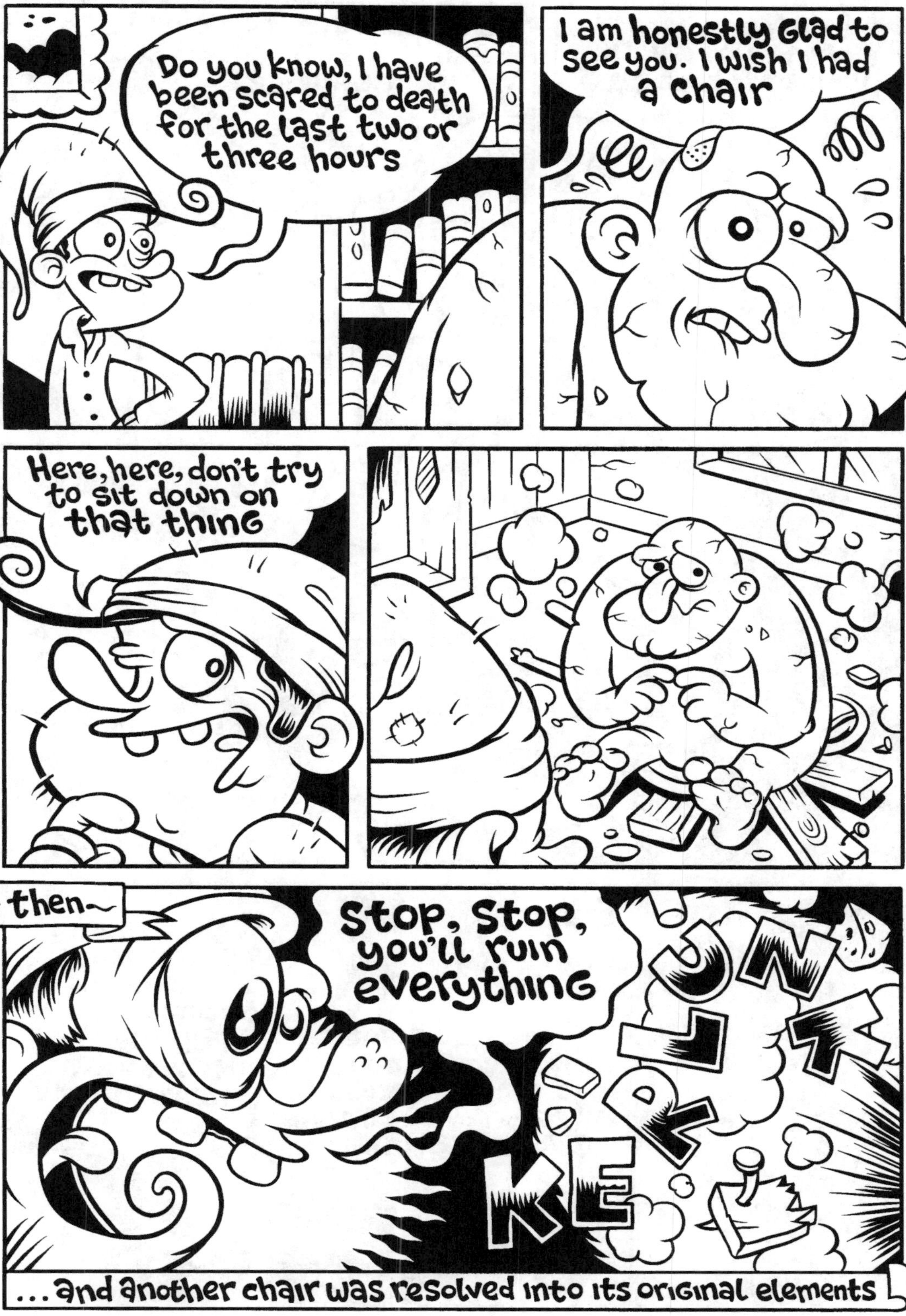
Do you know, I have been scared to death for the last two or three hours
I am honestly glad to see you. I wish I had a chair
Here, here, don't try to sit down on that thing
then~
Stop, stop, you'll ruin everything
KERPLUNK
...and another chair was resolved into its original elements

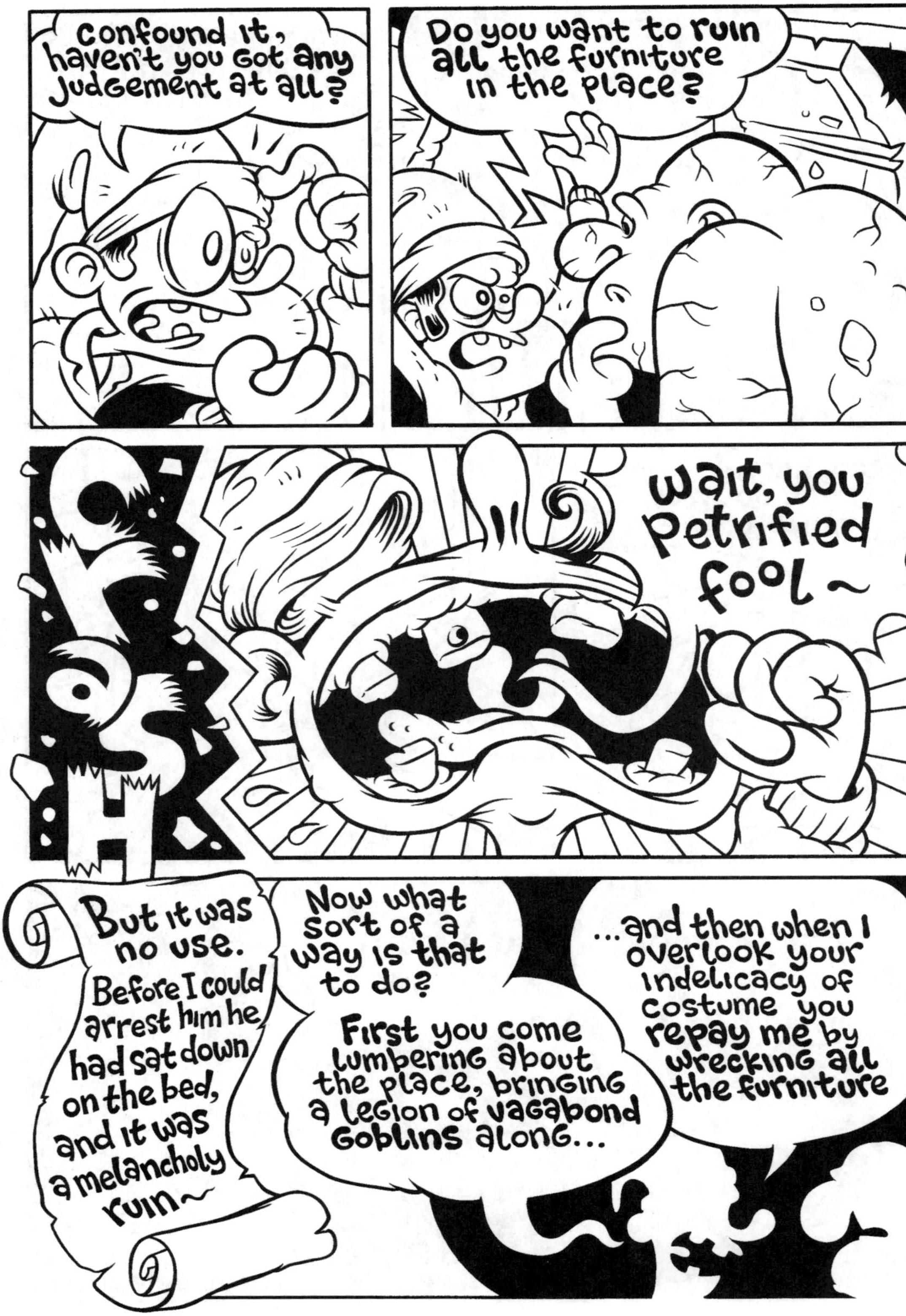
Confound it, haven't you got any judgement at all?
Do you want to ruin all the furniture in the place?
CRASH
Wait, you petrified fool~
But it was no use. Before I could arrest him he had sat down on the bed, and it was a melancholy ruin~
Now what sort of a way is that to do?
First you come lumbering about the place, bringing a legion of vagabond goblins along...
...and then when I overlook your indelicacy of costume you repay me by wrecking all the furniture

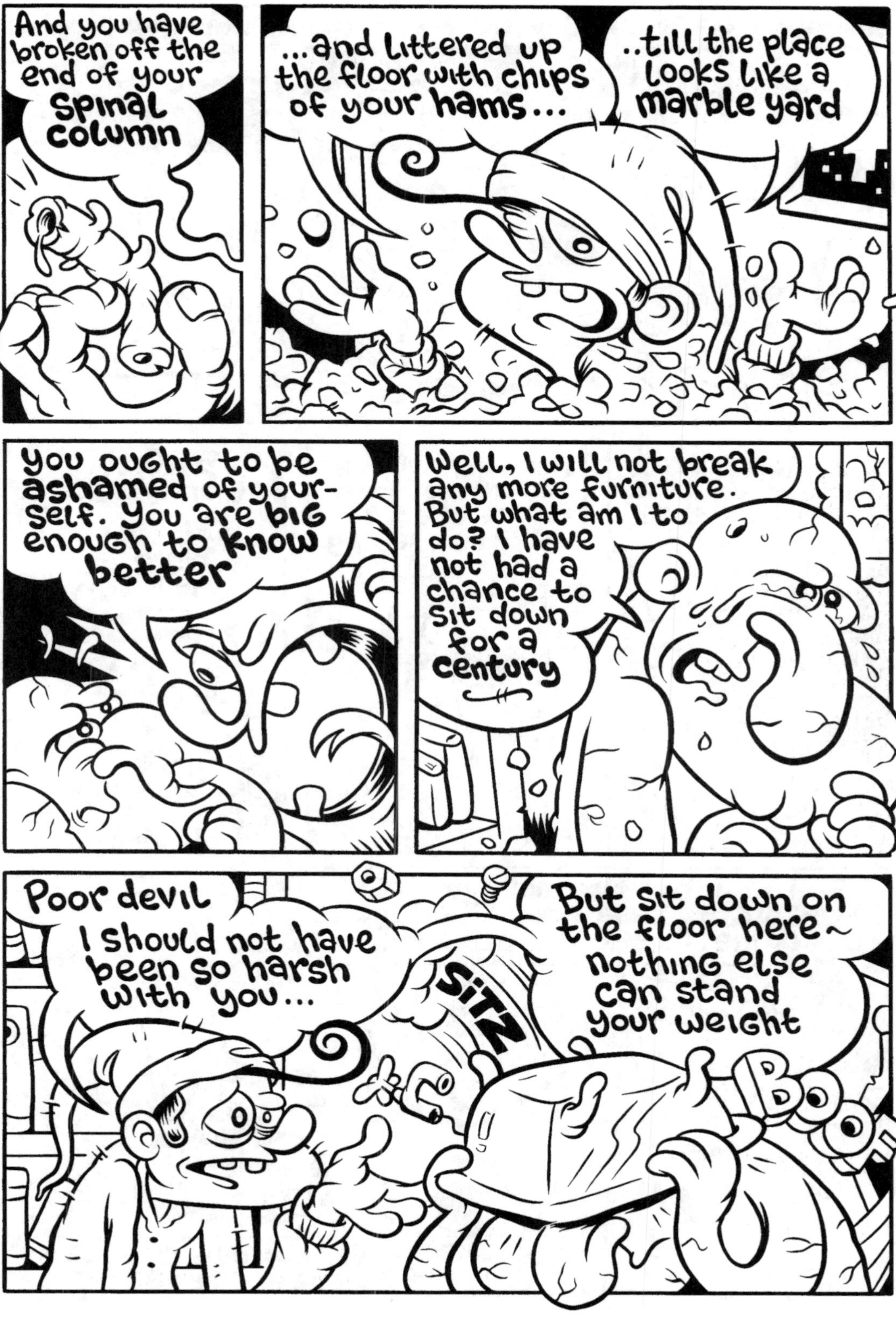
And you have broken off the end of your Spinal column
...and littered up the floor with chips of your hams...
..till the place looks like a marble yard
You ought to be ashamed of yourself. You are big enough to know better
Well, I will not break any more furniture. But what am I to do? I have not had a chance to sit down for a century
Poor devil
I should not have been so harsh with you...
But sit down on the floor here~ nothing else can stand your weight
SITZ
BOOM

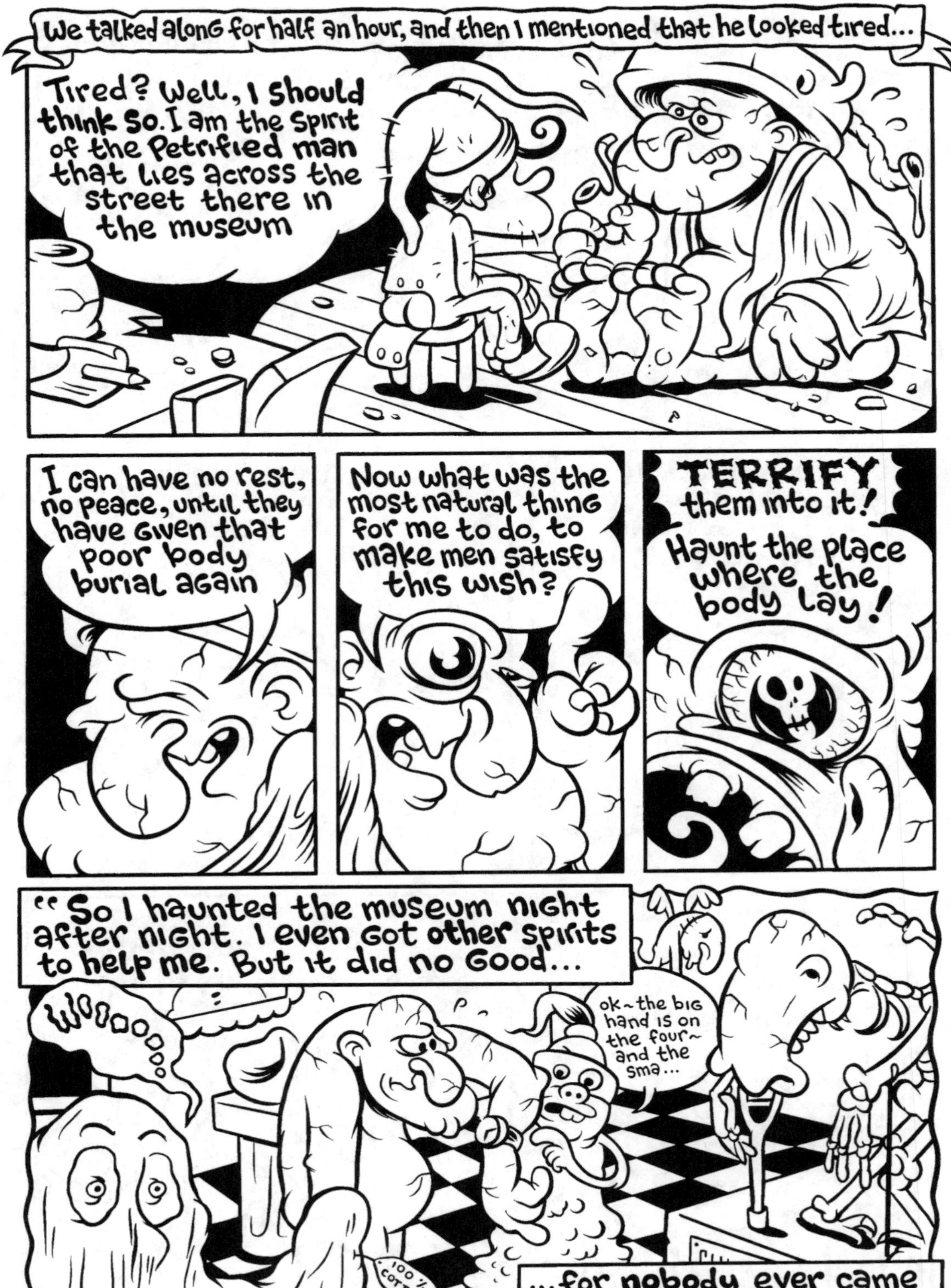
We talked along for half an hour, and then I mentioned that he looked tired...
Tired? Well, I should think so. I am the spirit of the Petrified man that lies across the street there in the museum
I can have no rest, no peace, until they have given that poor body burial again
Now what was the most natural thing for me to do, to make men satisfy this wish?
TERRIFY them into it!
Haunt the place where the body lay!
"So I haunted the museum night after night. I even got other spirits to help me. But it did no good...
Wooooooo
ok~the big hand is on the four~ and the sma...
100% COTTON
...for nobody ever came to the museum at night"

Then it occurred to me to come over and haunt **this place** a little

hoo0oooo

"Night after night we have shivered around through these mildewed halls, dragging chains, groaning, whispering, tramping up and down stairs, till, to tell you the truth, I am almost worn out"

"But when I saw a **light** in your room tonight, I **roused** my energies and went at it with a deal of the old freshness"

Now I am entirely **fagged out**

Give me, I beseech you, give me some hope!

Why you poor, blundering old **fossil**...

You have had all your trouble for **nothing**...

You have been haunting a **PLASTER CAST** of yourself ~ the **real** Cardiff Giant is in **Syracuse!**

Honestly, is that **true**?

As true as I am sitting here

Well ~ I never felt so absurd before. The Petrified man has sold everybody else, and **now** the mean fraud has ended by selling its **own ghost!**

My son, if there is any charity left in your heart for a poor friendless phantom like me, don't let this get out

Think of how **you** would feel if you had made such an **ass** of yourself

I heard him tramp step by step down the stairs and out into the deserted street, and felt sorry that he was gone, poor fellow...

THUD THUMP

...and sorrier still that he had carried off my blanket and my bathtub

©2004 ANTON EMDIN

My father was a St. Bernard, my mother was a collie, but I am a Presbyterian.

This is what my mother told me, I do not know these nice distinctions myself. To me they are only fine large words meaning nothing.

The UHURU-KAI (Free-Life) FAMILY THEATRE presents: A DOG'S TALE by Mark Twain (Samuel Clemens)

She was of a rather vain and frivolous character; still, she had a kind heart and gentle ways, and never harbored resentments for injuries done her, but put them easily out of her mind and forgot them; and she taught her children her kindly way, and from her we learned also to be brave and prompt in time of danger, and not to run away, but face the peril that threatened friend or stranger, and help him the best we could without stopping to think what the cost might be to us. And she taught us not by words only, but by example, and that is the best way and the surest and the most lasting. So, as you see, there was more to her than her education.

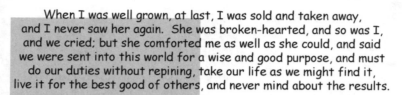

When I was well grown, at last, I was sold and taken away, and I never saw her again. She was broken-hearted, and so was I, and we cried; but she comforted me as well as she could, and said we were sent into this world for a wise and good purpose, and must do our duties without repining, take our life as we might find it, live it for the best good of others, and never mind about the results.

She said men who did like this would have a noble and beautiful reward by and by in another world, and although we animals would not go there, to do well and right without reward would give to our brief lives a worthiness and dignity which in itself would be a reward. She had gathered these things from time to time when she had gone to the Sunday-school with the children, and had laid them up in her memory.

So we said our farewells, and looked our last upon each other through our tears; and the last thing she said --keeping it for the last to make me remember it the better, I think--was, "In memory of me, when there is a time of danger to another do not think of yourself, think of your mother, and do as she would do."

Do you think I could forget that?

No.

My new home was a fine house,
with pictures, and
a great garden.

Mrs. Gray was thirty, and
sweet and lovely, and Sadie was
ten, just a darling little copy of
her mother, and the baby was a
year old, and fond of me, and
never could get enough of
hauling on my tail, and
hugging me, and laughing out
its innocent happiness; and
Mr. Gray was thirty-eight, and
tall and slender and handsome,
a renowned scientist.

I do not know what the
word means, but that is
not the best one; the
best word was
laboratory.

The laboratory was not a book, or
a picture, or a place to wash your
hands in, no, that is the lavatory;
the laboratory is filled with jars,
and bottles, and electrics, and
wires, and strange machines;
and every week other scientists
came there and sat in the place,
and used the machines,
and discussed, and made what
they called experiments and
discoveries; and often I came,
too, and stood around and
listened, and tried to learn, for
the sake of my mother, and in
loving memory of her.

Other times I lay on the floor in the mistress's workroom and slept,
she gently using me for a footstool, knowing it pleased me,
for it was a caress; other times I spent an hour in the nursery,
and got well tousled and made happy; other times I watched by the
crib there, when the baby was asleep and the nurse out for a few
minutes on the baby's affairs.

And so, as you see, mine was
a pleasant life.
There could not be a happier dog
than I was, nor a gratefuler one.
I will say this for myself, for it is only
the truth: I tried in all ways to do
well and right, and honor my mother's
memory and her teachings,
and earn the happiness that had come
to me, as best I could.

By and by came my little puppy,
and then my cup was full,
my happiness was perfect.
It was the dearest little
waddling thing, and so smooth
and soft and velvety,
and had such cunning little
awkward paws,
and such affectionate eyes,
and such a sweet and
innocent face.

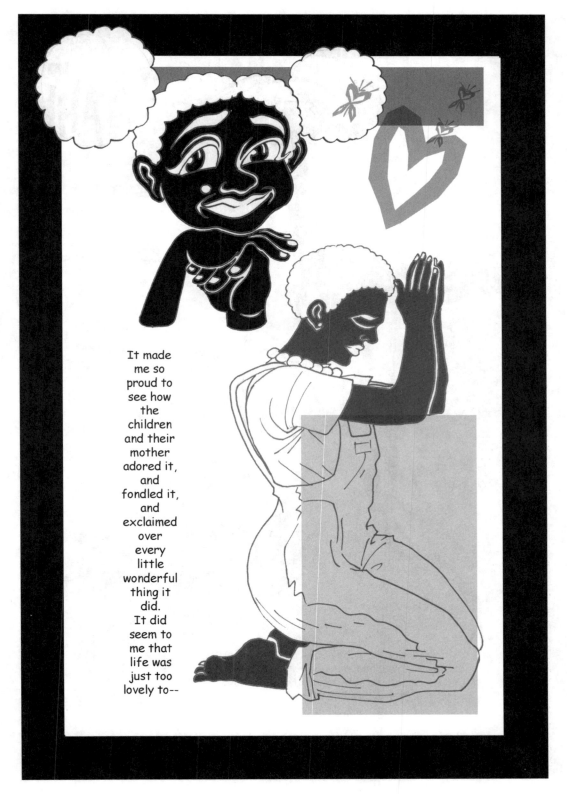

It made me so proud to see how the children and their mother adored it, and fondled it, and exclaimed over every little wonderful thing it did. It did seem to me that life was just too lovely to--

Then came the winter.

One day while I was standing watch in the nursery, a spark from the wood fire suddenly lit the bed ablaze.

A scream from the baby awoke me, and before I could think, I reached my head through the flames and dragged the baby out by the waistband, and tugged it along, and we fell to the floor together in a cloud of smoke;

I snatched a new hold, and dragged the screaming little creature along and out at the door and around the bend of the hall, and was still tugging away, all excited and happy and proud, when the master's voice shouted:

"Begone you cursed beast!"

I jumped to save myself; but he was furiously quick, and chased me up, striking furiously at me with his cane, I dodging this way and that, in terror, and at last a strong blow fell upon my left foreleg, which made me shriek and fall, for the moment,

the cane went up for another blow, but never descended, for the nurse's voice rang wildly out, "The nursery's on fire!" and the master rushed away in that direction, and my other bones were saved.

The pain was cruel, but, no matter, I must not lose any time; he might come back at any moment; so I limped on three legs to the other end of the hall, where there was a dark little stairway leading up into a garret where people seldom went. I managed to climb up there, then I searched my way among the piles of things, and hid in the secretest place I could find. It was foolish to be afraid there, yet still I was; so afraid that I hardly even whimpered, though it would have been such a comfort to whimper, because that eases the pain, you know. But I could lick my leg, and that did some good.

For half an hour there was a commotion downstairs, and shoutings, and rushing foot-steps, and then there was quiet again. Then came a sound that froze me. They were calling me--calling me.

It was muffled by distance, but that could not take the terror out of it, and it was the most dreadful sound to me that I had ever heard. I thought it would never, never stop. But at last it did, hours and hours after the vague twilight of the garret had long ago been blotted out by black darkness.

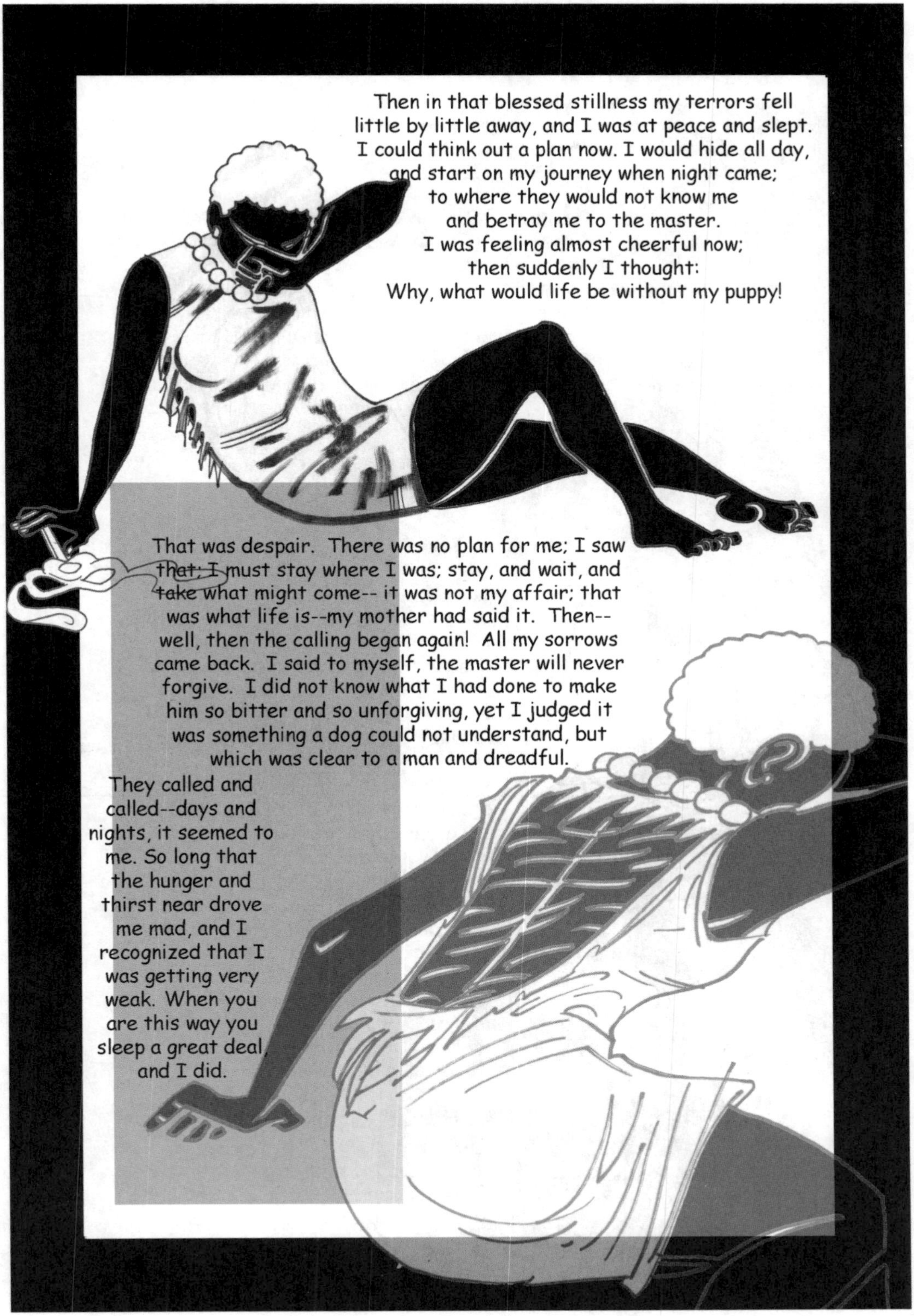

Then in that blessed stillness my terrors fell little by little away, and I was at peace and slept. I could think out a plan now. I would hide all day, and start on my journey when night came; to where they would not know me and betray me to the master. I was feeling almost cheerful now; then suddenly I thought: Why, what would life be without my puppy!

That was despair. There was no plan for me; I saw that; I must stay where I was; stay, and wait, and take what might come-- it was not my affair; that was what life is--my mother had said it. Then-- well, then the calling began again! All my sorrows came back. I said to myself, the master will never forgive. I did not know what I had done to make him so bitter and so unforgiving, yet I judged it was something a dog could not understand, but which was clear to a man and dreadful.

They called and called--days and nights, it seemed to me. So long that the hunger and thirst near drove me mad, and I recognized that I was getting very weak. When you are this way you sleep a great deal, and I did.

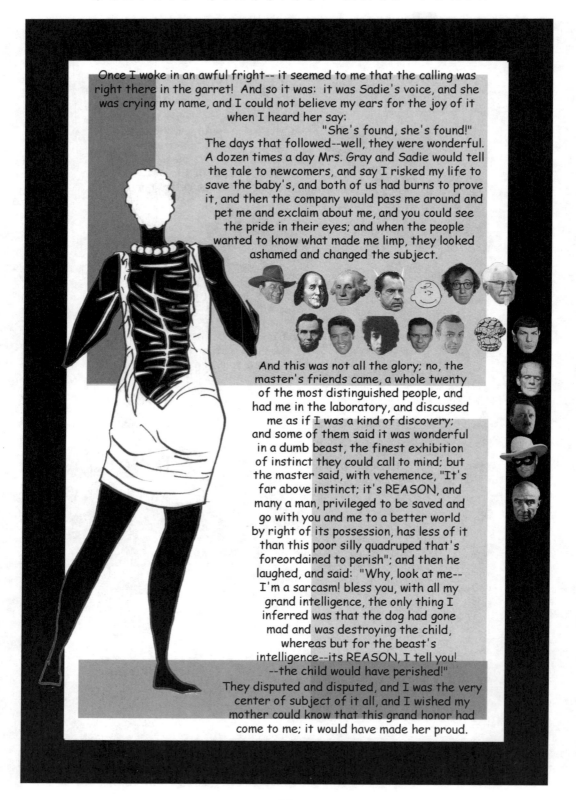

Once I woke in an awful fright-- it seemed to me that the calling was right there in the garret! And so it was: it was Sadie's voice, and she was crying my name, and I could not believe my ears for the joy of it when I heard her say:
"She's found, she's found!"
The days that followed--well, they were wonderful. A dozen times a day Mrs. Gray and Sadie would tell the tale to newcomers, and say I risked my life to save the baby's, and both of us had burns to prove it, and then the company would pass me around and pet me and exclaim about me, and you could see the pride in their eyes; and when the people wanted to know what made me limp, they looked ashamed and changed the subject.

And this was not all the glory; no, the master's friends came, a whole twenty of the most distinguished people, and had me in the laboratory, and discussed me as if I was a kind of discovery; and some of them said it was wonderful in a dumb beast, the finest exhibition of instinct they could call to mind; but the master said, with vehemence, "It's far above instinct; it's REASON, and many a man, privileged to be saved and go with you and me to a better world by right of its possession, has less of it than this poor silly quadruped that's foreordained to perish"; and then he laughed, and said: "Why, look at me-- I'm a sarcasm! bless you, with all my grand intelligence, the only thing I inferred was that the dog had gone mad and was destroying the child, whereas but for the beast's intelligence--its REASON, I tell you! --the child would have perished!"
They disputed and disputed, and I was the very center of subject of it all, and I wished my mother could know that this grand honor had come to me; it would have made her proud.

Then they discussed optics, as they called it, and whether a certain injury to the brain would produce blindness or not, but they could not agree about it, and said they must test it by experiment by and by; and next they discussed plants, and that interested me, because in the summer Sadie and I had planted seeds--I helped her dig the holes, you know--and after days and days a little shrub or a flower came up there, and it was a wonder how that could happen; but it did, and I wished I could talk--I would have told those people about it and shown then how much I knew, and been all alive with the subject; but I didn't care for the optics; it was dull, and when they came back to it again it bored me, and I went to sleep.

And one day those men came again, and said, now for the test, and they took the puppy to the laboratory, and I limped three-leggedly along, too, feeling proud, for any attention shown

They discussed and experimented, and then suddenly the puppy shrieked, and they set her on the floor, and she went staggering around, with her head all bloody, and the master clapped his hands and shouted:

"There, I've won--confess it!

And they all said:

"It's so--you've proved your theory, and suffering humanity owes you a great debt from henceforth," and they crowded around him, and wrung his hand cordially and thankfully, and praised him.

But I hardly saw or heard these things, for I ran at once to my little darling, and snuggled close to it where it lay, and licked the blood, and it put its head against mine, whimpering softly, and I knew in my heart it was a comfort to it in its pain and trouble to feel its mother's touch, though it could not see me.

Then it dropped down, presently, and its little velvet nose rested upon the floor, and it was still, and did not move any more.

Soon the master stopped discuss-
ing a moment, and rang in the
footman, and said,
"Bury it in the far corner of the
garden," and then went
on with the discussion, and I
trotted after the footman, very
happy and grateful, for I knew
the puppy was out of its pain now,
because it was asleep.

We went far down the garden
to the farthest end, where the
children and the nurse and the
puppy and I used to play
in the summer in the shade of a
great elm, and there the footman
dug a hole, and I saw he was going
to plant the puppy, and I was
glad, because it would grow and
come up a fine handsome dog,
and be a beautiful surprise for
the family when they came home;
so I tried to help him dig, but my
lame leg was no good, being stiff,
you know, and you have to have
two, or it is no use.

When the
footman had finished and covered
my little one up, he patted my
head, and there were tears in his
eyes, and he said:

"Poor little doggie,
you saved HIS child!"

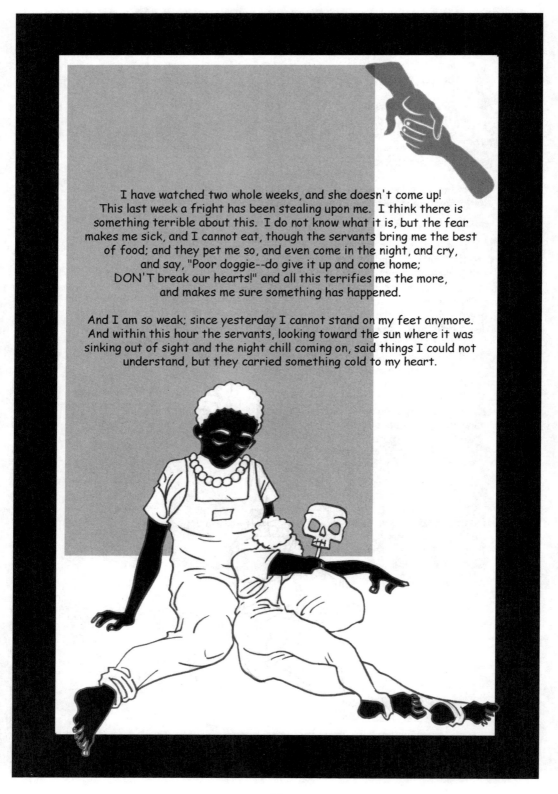

I have watched two whole weeks, and she doesn't come up!
This last week a fright has been stealing upon me. I think there is
something terrible about this. I do not know what it is, but the fear
makes me sick, and I cannot eat, though the servants bring me the best
of food; and they pet me so, and even come in the night, and cry,
and say, "Poor doggie--do give it up and come home;
DON'T break our hearts!" and all this terrifies me the more,
and makes me sure something has happened.

And I am so weak; since yesterday I cannot stand on my feet anymore.
And within this hour the servants, looking toward the sun where it was
sinking out of sight and the night chill coming on, said things I could not
understand, but they carried something cold to my heart.

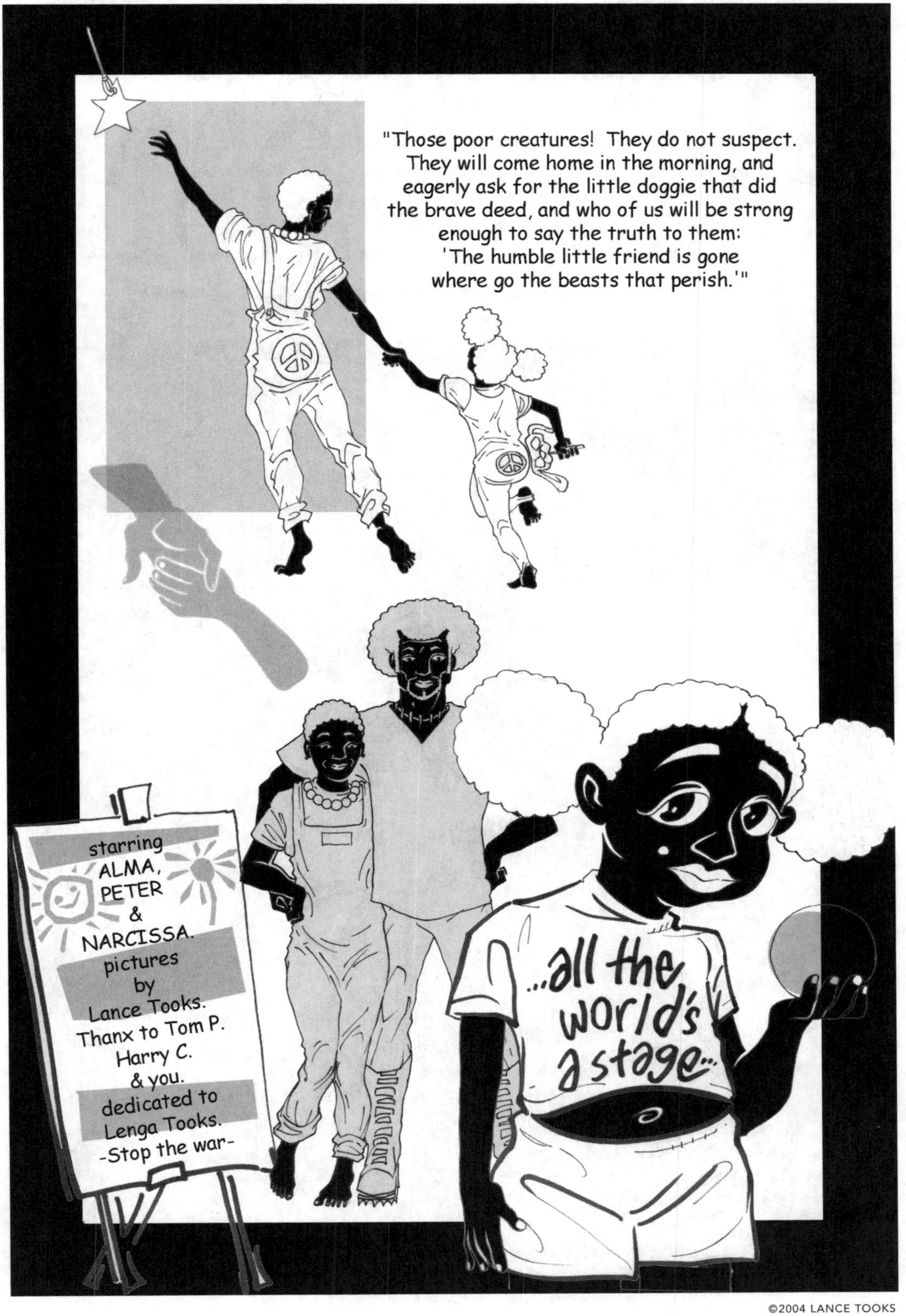
"Those poor creatures! They do not suspect. They will come home in the morning, and eagerly ask for the little doggie that did the brave deed, and who of us will be strong enough to say the truth to them: 'The humble little friend is gone where go the beasts that perish.'"
starring ALMA, PETER & NARCISSA.
pictures by Lance Tooks.
Thanx to Tom P. Harry C. & you.
dedicated to Lenga Tooks.
-Stop the war-
...all the world's a stage...

A CURIOUS PLEASURE EXCURSION

Being a Public Service Announcement by **Mark Twain**

THIS IS TO INFORM **THE PUBLIC** *that as of* JUNE 1, 1874

in connection with **MR. P. T. BARNUM** *I have leased the* **CELESTIAL BODY**

Known as **COGGIA'S COMET** and

I DESIRE to solicit the **PUBLIC PATRONAGE** in favor of a **BENEFICIAL ENTERPRISE** *which we have in view.*

Illustrated by **William L. Brown**

WE PROPOSE

To FIT UP

COMFORTABLE, And

Even **LUXURIOUS,**

ACCOMMODATIONS In The

TAIL OF THE COMET

FOR As Many PERSONS

As Will HONOR Us *WITH* Their PATRONAGE,

And MAKE AN EXTENDED EXCURSION AMONG

THE HEAVENLY BODIES.

The *COMET* Will Leave *NEW YORK*

At 10 P.M. On The 20TH OF JUNE,

and *THEREFORE* it will be DESIRABLE

That The PASSENGERS Be *ON BOARD*

BY **EIGHT AT THE LATEST**

To Avoid Confusion In Getting Under Way

NO DOGS WILL BE ALLOWED ON BOARD.

We Shall Have

BILLIARD Rooms,

CARD Rooms,

MUSIC Rooms,

BOWLING ALLEYS

and Spacious THEATERS

and LIBRARIES;

And On The MAIN DECK We Propose To Have

A DRIVING PARK,

With Upward Of

100,000 MILES OF ROADWAY.

Meals Served In Staterooms Charged Extra.

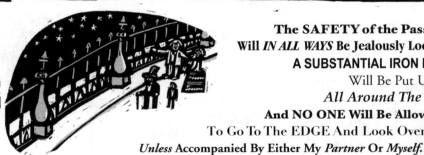

**The SAFETY of the Passengers
Will *IN ALL WAYS* Be Jealously Looked To.
A SUBSTANTIAL IRON RAILING**
Will Be Put Up
All Around The Comet,
And NO ONE Will Be Allowed
To Go To The EDGE And Look Over
Unless Accompanied By Either My *Partner* Or *Myself.*

**Hostility Is Not Apprehended
From Any INHABITANTS OF THE STARS,**
But We Have Thought It Best To Err On The SAFE Side,
And *Therefore* Have Provided Sufficient
ARMAMENTS, Including *A Proper Number* Of
MORTARS, SIEGE GUNS, *And* **BOARDING PIKES.**

We Shall Hope To leave a
GOOD IMPRESSION OF AMERICA
Behind Us *But* **At The Same Time**
We Shall **PROMPTLY** *Resent* Any *Injury*
That May Be Done Us *Or* Any *Insolence* Offered Us,
By *PARTIES* or *GOVERNMENTS*
Residing In **ANY STAR** *In The Firmament.*

**We Shall Take With Us A GREAT FORCE
Of MISSIONARIES,** And *Shed The True Light*
Upon The **CELESTIAL ORBS** Which,
Physically Aglow, Are Yet *Morally In Darkness.*
SUNDAY SCHOOLS And **COMPULSORY EDUCATION**
Will Be Established *Wherever Practicable.*

The *Comet* Will Visit *MARS* first,
And proceed to
MERCURY, JUPITER,
VENUS, and SATURN.
Every STAR of *Prominent Magnitude*,
And Every Constellation Of Importance
Will Be Visited, With Time Allowed For
EXCURSIONS To *Points Of Interest* Inland.

First-Class Fare Will Be Charged
At *The Low Rate* Of $2
For *Every* 50,000,000 Miles Of *Actual Travel*.
Passengers Desiring To Diverge
AT ANY POINT
Will Be Transferred To Other Comets.
We *Will* Make *Connections*
AT PRINCIPAL POINTS
With All Reliable Lines.

Passengers Paying Double Fare
Will Be *Entitled* To A Share
In All The New
Stars, Suns, Moons, And Meteors
We May Discover.
Advertisers Will Take Notice
That We Will Carry *Billboards* Along
For **Use** In The **Constellations**,
And Are Open To Terms.

For Further Particulars, Apply On Board, Or To My Partner, But Not
To Me, Since I Do Not Take Charge Of The Comet Until She Is Under
Way. It Is Necessary, At A Time Like This, That My Mind Should Not Be
Burdened With Small Business Details.

-Mark Twain

A REMINISCENCE
OF THE BACK
SETTLEMENTS

by Mark Twain
illustrated by Lisa K. Weber

NOW THAT CORPSE (said the undertaker, patting the folded hands of the deceased approvingly) was a brick—every way you took him he was a brick. He was so real accommodating, and so modest-like and simple in his last moments. Friends wanted metallic burial case—nothing else would do. I couldn't get it. There warn't going to be time anybody could see that. Corpse said never mind, shake him up some kind of a box he could stretch out in comfortable, he warn't particular 'bout the general style of it. Said he went more on room than style, any way, in the last final container. Friends wanted a silver doorplate on the coffin, signifying who he was and wher' he was from. Now you know a fellow couldn't roust out such a gaily thing as that in a little country town like this. What did corpse say? Corpse said, whitewash his old canoe and dob his address and general destination onto it with a blacking brush and a stencil plate, long with a verse from some likely hymn or other, and pint him for the tomb, and mark him C.O.D., and just let him skip along. He warn't distressed any more than you be—on the contrary just as carm and collected as a hearse-horse; said he judged that wher' he was going to, a body would find it considerable better to attract attention by a picturesque moral character than a natty burial case with a swell doorplate on it. Splendid man, he was. I'd druther do for a corpse like that 'n any I've tackled in seven year. There's some satisfaction in buryin' a man like that. You feel that what you're doing is appreciated. Lord bless you, so's he got planted before he sp'iled, he was perfectly satisfied; said his relations meant well, perfectly well, but all them preparations was bound to delay the thing more or less, and he didn't wish to be kept layin' round. You never see such a clear head as what he had—and so carm and so cool. Just a hunk of brains that is what he was. Perfectly awful. It was a ripping distance from one end of that man's head to t'other. Often and over again he's had brain fever a-raging in one place, and the rest of the pile didn't know anything about it—didn't affect it any more than an Injun insurrection in Arizona affects the Atlantic States. Well, the relations they wanted a big funeral, but corpse said he was down on flummery—didn't want any procession—fill the hearse full of mourners, and get out a stern line and tow him behind. He was the most down on style of any remains I ever struck. A beautiful, simple-minded creature—it was what he was, you can depend on that. He was just set on having things the way he wanted them, and he took a solid comfort in laying his little plans. He had me measure him and take a whole raft of directions; then he had a minister stand up behind a long box with a tablecloth over it and read his funeral sermon, saying 'Angcore, angcore!' at the good places, and making him scratch out every bit of brag about him, and all the hifalutin; and then he made them trot out the choir so's he could help them pick out the tunes for the occasion, and he got them to sing 'Pop Goes the Weasel,' because he'd always liked that tune when he was downhearted, and solemn music made him sad; and when they sung that with tears in their eyes (because they all loved him), and his relations grieving around, he just laid there as happy as a bug, and trying to beat time and showing all over how much he enjoyed it; and presently he got worked up and excited; and tried to join in, for mind you he was pretty proud of his abilities in the singing line; but the first time he opened his mouth and was just going to spread himself, his breath took a walk. I never see a man snuffed out so sudden. Ah, it was a great loss—it was a powerful loss to this poor little one-horse town. Well, well, well, I hain't got time to be palavering along here—got to nail on the lid and mosey along with him; and if you'll just give me a lift we'll skeet him into the hearse and meander along. Relations bound to have it so—don't pay no attention to dying injunctions, minute a corpse's gone; but if I had my way, if I didn't respect his last wishes and tow him behind the hearse, I'll be cuss'd. I consider that whatever a corpse wants done for his comfort is a little enough matter, and a man hain't got no right to deceive him or take advantage of him—and whatever a corpse trusts me to do I'm a-going to do, you know, even if it's to stuff him and paint him yaller and keep him for a keepsake—you hear me!"

He cracked his whip and went lumbering away with his ancient ruin of a hearse, and I continued my walk with a valuable lesson learned—that a healthy and wholesome cheerfulness is not necessarily impossible to any occupation. The lesson is likely to be lasting, for it will take many months to obliterate the memory of the remarks and circumstances that impressed it.

Is He Living Or Is He Dead?

A story by Mark Twain

Illustrated by Simon Gane

I was spending the month of March 1892 in Menton, on the Riviera. At this retired spot one has all the advantages which are to be had at Monte Carlo and Nice, without the fuss and feathers. Menton is quiet, unpretentious; now and then a rich man comes, and I presently got acquainted with one of these. I will call him Smith.

One day, at breakfast, he exclaimed:

Quick! Cast your eye on the man going out at the door.

Why? Do you know who he is?

Yes. He spent several days here before you came. He is a retired, and very rich, silk manufacturer from Lyon, they say, and I guess he is alone in the world, for he always looks sad and dreamy, and doesn't talk with anybody. His name is Theophile Magnan.

I supposed that Smith would now proceed to justify the large interest which he had shown in Monsieur Magnan, but, instead, he began to tell one of Hans Andersen's little stories:

"A child has a caged bird which it loves but thoughtlessly neglects. The bird pours out its song unheard and unheeded; but in time, hunger and thirst assail the creature, and finally, it dies.

"The child comes, is smitten with remorse, and buries the bird with elaborate pomp and the tenderest grief, without knowing that it isn't children only who starve poets to death and then spend enough on their funerals and monuments to have kept them alive and made them easy and comfortable."

I will now tell you a curious history. It has been a secret for many years - a secret between me and three others; but I am going to break the seal.

A long time ago I was a young artist. I wandered about France, sketching, and was presently joined by a couple of young Frenchmen who were doing much the same thing.

"Claude Frère

"and Carl Boulanger...

"dear fellows, and the sunniest souls who ever laughed at poverty.

"At last, an artist as poor as ourselves took us in and literally saved us from starving—

"François Millet."

What! The great François Millet?

"He wasn't any greater than we were, then. He was so poor that he had nothing to feed us on but turnips. We four became fast friends. We painted together, piling up stock, but very seldom getting rid of any of it. We had lovely times together; but how we were pinched!

"For a little over two years this went on. At last, one day, Claude said:

Boys, we've come to the end. I've been all around the village and they all refuse to credit us for another centime until all the debts are paid up.

We realized that our circumstances were desperate now. Carl said:

It's a shame! Look at these canvases: stacks of pictures as good as anybody in Europe paints - and plenty of strangers have said the same.

But didn't buy.

No matter, they said it; and it's true. Look at your ANGELUS there!

Pah! I was offered five francs for it.

Why didn't you take it?

I thought he would give more—so I asked him eight.

Well—and then?

He said he would call again.

Why, François—

Oh, I know! It was a mistake, and I was a fool.

Well don't be a fool again.

I wish somebody would come along and offer us a cabbage for it—you'd see!

A cabbage! Oh, don't name it—it makes my mouth water.

"'Boys,' said Carl, 'do these pictures lack merit? Answer me that.'"

NO!

If an illustrious name were attached to them they would sell at splendid prices. Isn't that so?

107

Certainly it is. How does that concern us?

In this way, comrades— we'll attach an illustrious name to them!

"The conversation stopped. The faces turned inquiringly upon Carl. He sat down, and said:

Now, I have a perfectly serious thing to propose. I think it is the only way to keep us out of the almshouse, and I believe my project will make us all rich.

Rich! You've lost your mind.

No, I haven't.

Carl, you want to take a pill and get right to bed.

Bandage him first — bandage his head and then—

Shut up!

Let the boy have his say. Now then — come out with your project, Carl. What is it?

Well, I will ask you to note this fact in human history: that the merit of many a great artist has never been acknowledged until after he was starved and dead. Then his pictures climb to high prices after his death. My project is this: we must cast lots— one of us must die.

108

"There was a wild chorus of advice for the help of Carl's brain; but he waited for the hilarity to calm down, and then went on again:

Yes, one of us must die. We will cast lots. The one chosen shall be illustrious, all of us shall be rich.

During the next three months the one who is to die shall paint with all his might, enlarge his stock all he can - sketches, studies, fragments of studies, a dozen dabs of the brush on each - turn out fifty a day, each to contain some peculiarity or mannerism easily detectable as his - they're the things that are collected at fabulous prices after the great man is gone; we'll have a ton of them ready!

And all that time the rest of us will be working Paris and the dealers.

You get the idea?

But about this dying-

Don't you see? The man doesn't really die; he changes his name and vanishes; we bury a dummy and cry over it, with all the world to help.

"Everybody jumped up in joy and broke out into applause. For hours we talked over the great plan, and at last, when all the details had been arranged, we cast lots...

"...and Millet was elected to die.

"Next morning, we left a stake of turnips for Millet to live on for a few days and the three of us cleared out, on foot."

Each of us carried a dozen of Millet's small pictures, purposing to market them. Carl struck for Paris, where he would start the work of building up Millet's name against the coming great day. Claude and I were to separate, and scatter abroad over France.

"I walked two days before I began business. Then I began to sketch a villa in the outskirts of a big town — because I saw the proprietor standing on the veranda. He came down to look on, and said I was a master!

"I put down my brush, reached into my satchel, fetched out a Millet, and pointed to the cipher in the corner, I said proudly:

Well, he taught me! I should think I ought to know my trade!

J.F. Millet

"The man looked embarrassed, and I said Sorrowfully:

You don't mean to intimate that you don't know the cipher of François Millet!

"Of course he didn't know that cipher; but he said:

Why, it is Millet's, sure enough! Of course I recognize it now.

Next, he wanted to buy it; and at last, I let him have it for eight hundred francs.

Eight hundred!

Yes. Millet would have sold it for a pork chop. I wish I could get it back for eighty thousand.

But that time's gone by. I made a very nice picture of that man's house and seeing as I was the pupil of such a master, I sold it to him for a hundred francs. I sent the eight hundred to Millet and struck out again next day.

"But I didn't walk—no. I rode. I have ridden ever since. I sold one picture every day, and never tried to sell two. I always said to my customer:

I am a fool to sell a picture of François Millet's at all, for that man is not going to live three months, and when he dies his pictures can't be had for love or money.

"I took care to spread that little fact as far as I could, and prepare the world for the event. Claude and Carl were reporting equal success.

"Carl was soon in Paris and he made friends with the correspondents, and got Millet's condition reported all over the continent.

"Every now and then we got in with a country editor and started an item concerning the condition of the 'master'—always tinged with fears for the worst.

"At the end of six weeks, we three met in Paris and decided not to wait any longer. So we wrote Millet to go to bed and begin to waste away pretty fast, for we should like him to die in ten days.

"We had a champagne supper that night, and next day Claude and I went to nurse Millet through his last days and to send daily bulletins to Paris for publication in the papers of a waiting world.

"Then we figured up and found that among us we had sold eighty-five pictures, and had sixty-nine thousand francs to show for it.

"The sad end came at last, and Carl was there in time to help in the final mournful rites.

"You remember that great funeral, and what a stir it made all over the globe, and how the illustrious came to testify their sorrow."

We four carried the coffin, which hadn't anything in it but a wax figure, and—

But, which four?

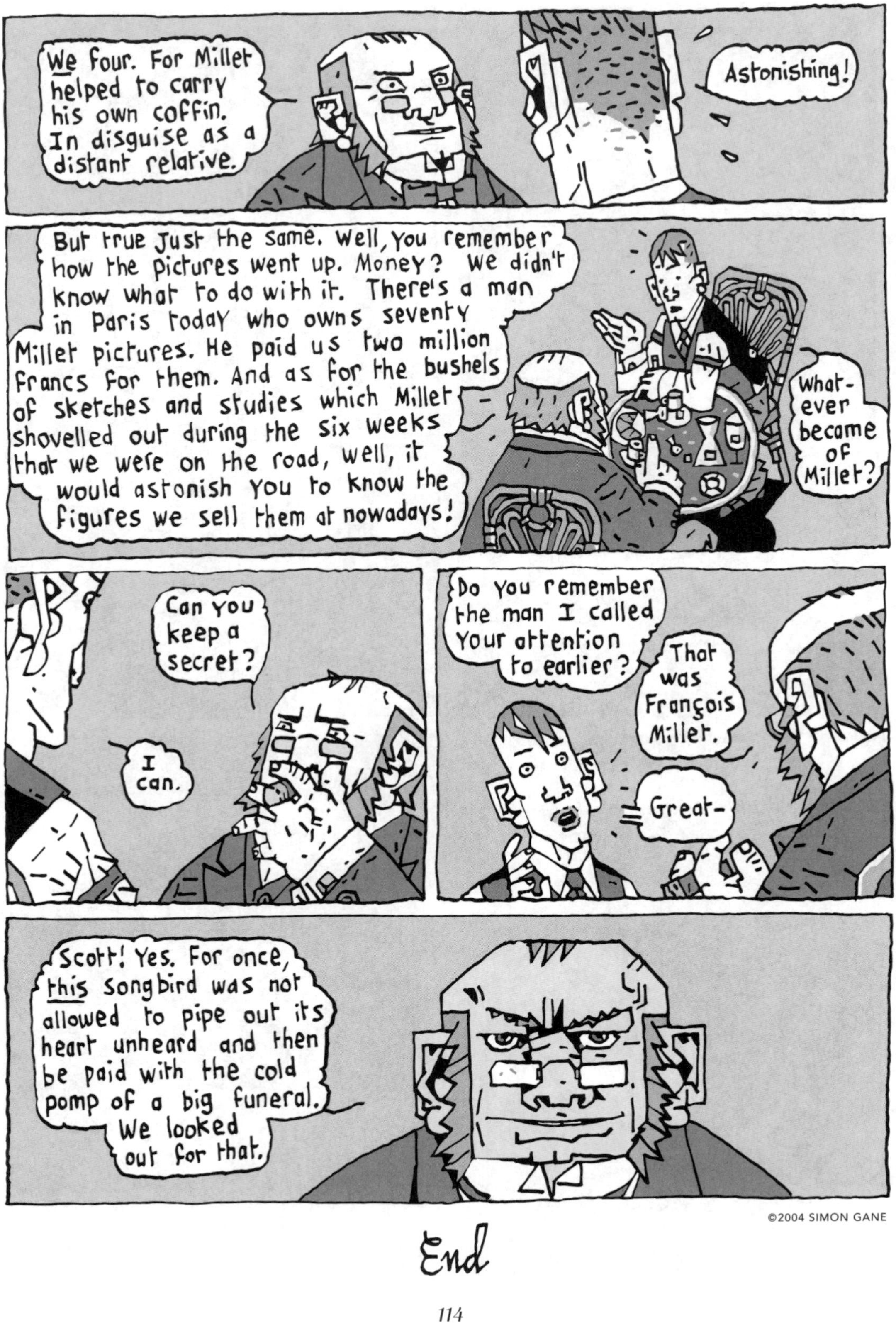
We four. For Millet helped to carry his own coffin. In disguise as a distant relative.
Astonishing!
But true just the same. Well, you remember how the pictures went up. Money? We didn't know what to do with it. There's a man in Paris today who owns seventy Millet pictures. He paid us two million francs for them. And as for the bushels of sketches and studies which Millet shovelled out during the six weeks that we were on the road, well, it would astonish you to know the figures we sell them at nowadays!
What-ever became of Millet?
Can you keep a secret?
I can.
Do you remember the man I called your attention to earlier?
That was François Millet.
Great-
Scott! Yes. For once, this songbird was not allowed to pipe out its heart unheard and then be paid with the cold pomp of a big funeral. We looked out for that.

End

Advice To Little Girls

BY **MARK TWAIN**

Good little girls always show marked deference for the aged.
You ought never to sass old people
unless they sass you first.

ILLUSTRATED BY **FLORENCE CESTAC**

Good little girls *ought not to make mouths at their teachers for every trifling offense. This retaliation should only be resorted to under peculiarly aggravated circumstances.*

ILLUSTRATED BY **KIRSTEN ULVE**

If your mother tells you to do a thing,
it is wrong to reply that you won't. It is better and more
becoming to intimate that you will do as she bids you, and then
afterward act quietly in the matter according to the dictates of
your best judgment.

ILLUSTRATED BY **SHARY FLENNIKEN**

If you have nothing but a rag-doll stuffed with sawdust, while one of your more fortunate little playmates has a costly China one, you should treat her with a show of kindness nevertheless. And you ought not to attempt to make a forcible swap with her unless your conscience would justify you in it, and you know you are able to do it.

ILLUSTRATED BY **TONI PAWLOWSKY**

If at any time you find it necessary to correct your brother,
do not correct him with mud—never, on any account, throw mud
at him, because it will spoil his clothes. It is better to scald him a
little, for then you obtain desirable results. You secure his immediate
attention to the lessons you are inculcating, and at the same time
your hot water will have a tendency to move impurities from his
person, and possibly the skin, in spots.

ILLUSTRATED BY **MARY FLEENER**

You ought never to take your little brother's chewing-gum away from him by main force; it is better to rope him in with the promise of the first two dollars and a half you find floating down the river on a grindstone. In the artless simplicity natural to this time of life, he will regard it as a perfectly fair transaction. In all ages of the world this eminently plausible fiction has lured the obtuse infant to financial ruin and disaster.

ILLUSTRATED BY **ANNIE OWENS**

You should ever bear in mind *that it is to your kind parents that you are indebted for your food, and for the privilege of staying home from school when you let on that you are sick. Therefore you ought to respect their little prejudices, and humor their little whims, and put up with their little foibles until they get to crowding you too much.*

ILLUSTRATED BY **LESLEY REPPETEAUX**

AN ENCOUNTER WITH AN INTERVIEWER

by **Mark Twain**

illustrated by **Skip Williamson**

The nervous, dapper young man took the chair I offered him, and said he was connected with the **Daily Thunderstorm**, and added:

"Hoping it's no harm, I've come to interview you."

"Come to what?"

"Interview you."

"Ah! I see. Yes—yes. Um! Yes—yes."

I was not feeling bright that morning. Indeed, my powers seemed a bit under a cloud. However, I went to the bookcase, and when I had been looking six or seven minutes I found I was obliged to refer to the young man. I said:

"How do you spell it?"

"Spell what?"

"Interview."

"Oh, my goodness! What do you want to spell it for?"

"I don't want to spell it; I want to see what it means."

"Well, this is astonishing, I must say. I can tell you what it means, if you—"

"Oh, all right! That will answer, and much obliged to you, too."

"In, in, ter, ter, inter—"

"Then you spell it with an I?"

"Why certainly!"

"Oh, that is what took me so long."

"Why, my dear sir, what did you propose to spell it with?"

"Well, I—I—hardly know. I had the Unabridged, and I was ciphering around in the back end, hoping I might tree her among the pictures. But it's a very old edition."

"Why, my friend, they wouldn't have a picture of it in even the latest e— My dear sir, I beg your pardon, I mean no harm in the world, but you do not look as—as—intelligent as I had expected you would. No harm—I mean no harm at all."

"Oh, don't mention it! It has often been said, and by people who would not flatter and who could have no inducement to flatter, that I am quite remarkable in that way. Yes—yes; they always speak of it with rapture."

"I can easily imagine it. But about this interview. You know it is the custom, now, to interview any man who has become notorious."

"Indeed, I had not heard of it before. It must be very interesting. What do you do it with?"

"Ah, well—well—well—this is disheartening. It ought to be done with a club in some cases; but customarily it consists in the interviewer asking questions and the interviewed answering them. It is all the rage now. Will you let me ask you certain questions calculated to bring out the salient points of your public and private history?"

"Oh, with pleasure—with pleasure. I have a very bad memory, but I hope you will not mind that. That is to say, it is an irregular memory— singularly irregular. Sometimes it goes in a gallop, and then again it will be as much as a fortnight passing a given point. This is a great grief to me."

"Oh, it is no matter, so you will try to do the best you can."

"I will. I will put my whole mind on it."

"Thank you. Are you ready to begin?"

"Ready."

Q. How old are you?
A. Nineteen, in June.
Q. Indeed. I would have taken you to be thirty-five or six. Where were you born?
A. In Missouri.
Q. When did you begin to write?
A. In 1836.
Q. Why, how could that be, if you are only nineteen now?
A. I don't know. It does seem curious, somehow.
Q. It does, indeed. Whom do you consider the most remarkable man you ever met?
A. Aaron Burr.
Q. But you never could have met Aaron Burr, if you are only nineteen years!
A. Now, if you know more about me than I do, what do you ask me for?
Q. Well, it was only a suggestion; nothing more. How did you happen to meet Burr?
A. Well, I happened to be at his funeral one day, and he asked me to make less noise, and—
Q. But, good heavens! if you were at his funeral, he must have been dead, and if he was dead how could he care whether you made a noise or not?
A. I don't know. He was always a particular kind of a man that way.
Q. Still, I don't understand it at all. You say he spoke to you, and that he was dead.

A. I didn't say he was dead.

Q. But wasn't he dead?

A. Well, some said he was, some said he wasn't.

Q. What did you think?

A. Oh, it was none of my business! It wasn't any of my funeral.

Q. Did you—However, we can never get this matter straight. Let me ask about something else. What was the date of your birth?

A. Monday, October 31, 1693.

Q. What! Impossible! That would make you a hundred and eighty years old. How do you account for that?

A. I don't account for it at all.

Q. But you said at first you were only nineteen, and now you make yourself out to be one hundred and eighty. It is an awful discrepancy.

A. Why, have you noticed that? (Shaking hands.) Many a time it has seemed to me like a discrepancy, but somehow I couldn't make up my mind. How quick you notice a thing!

Q. Thank you for the compliment, as far as it goes. Had you, or have you, any brothers or sisters?

A. Eh! I—I—I think so — yes — but I don't remember.

Q. Well, that is the most extraordinary statement I ever heard!

A. Why, what makes you think that?

Q. How could I think otherwise? Why, look here! Who is this a picture of on the wall? Isn't that a brother of yours?

A. Oh, yes, yes, yes! Now you remind me of it; that was a brother of mine. That's William — Bill we called him. Poor old Bill!

Q. Why? Is he dead, then?

A. Ah! well, I suppose so. We never could tell. There was a great mystery about it.

Q. That is sad, very sad. He disappeared, then?

A. Well, yes, in a sort of general way. We buried him.

Q. Buried him! Buried him, without knowing whether he was dead or not?

A. Oh, no! Not that. He was dead enough.

Q. Well, I confess that I can't understand this. If you buried him, and you knew he was dead—

A. No! no! We only thought he was.

Q. Oh, I see! He came to life again?

A. I bet he didn't.

Q. Well, I never heard anything like this. Somebody was dead. Somebody was buried. Now, where was the mystery?

A. Ah! that's just it! That's it exactly. You see, we were twins — defunct — and I — and we got mixed in the bathtub when we were only two weeks old, and one of us was drowned. But we didn't know which. Some think it was Bill. Some think it was me.

Q. Well, that is remarkable. What do you think?

A. Goodness knows! I would give whole worlds to know. This solemn, this awful mystery has cast a gloom over my whole life. But I will tell you a secret now, which I never have revealed to any creature before. One of us had a peculiar mark — a large mole on the back of his left hand; that was me. That child was the one that was drowned!

Q. Very well, then, I don't see that there is any mystery about it, after all.

A. You don't? Well, I do. Anyway, I don't see how they could ever have been such a blundering lot as to go and bury the wrong child. But, 'sh!— don't mention it where the family can hear of it. Heaven knows they have heartbreaking troubles enough without adding this.

Q. Well, I believe I have got material enough for the present, and I am very much obliged to you for the pains you have taken. But I was a good deal interested in that account of Aaron Burr's funeral. Would you mind telling me what particular circumstance it was that made you think Burr was such a remarkable man?

A. Oh! It was a mere trifle! Not one man in fifty would have noticed it at all. When the sermon was over, and the procession all ready to start for the cemetery, and the body all arranged nice in the hearse, he said he wanted to take a last look at the scenery, and so he got up and rode with the driver.

Then the young man reverently withdrew. He was very pleasant company, and I was sorry to see him go.

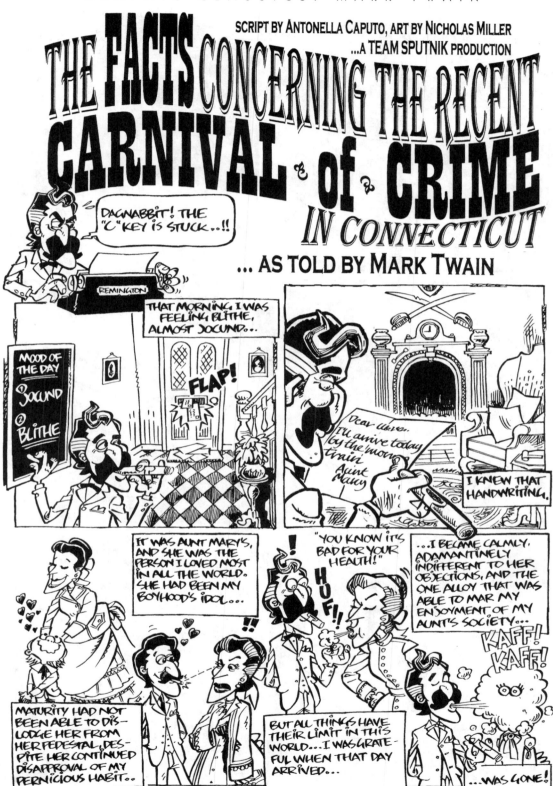

SCRIPT BY ANTONELLA CAPUTO, ART BY NICHOLAS MILLER
...A TEAM SPUTNIK PRODUCTION

THE FACTS CONCERNING THE RECENT CARNIVAL of CRIME IN CONNECTICUT

... AS TOLD BY MARK TWAIN

DAGNABBIT! THE "C" KEY IS STUCK..!!

THAT MORNING I WAS FEELING BLITHE, ALMOST JOCUND...

MOOD OF THE DAY
① JOCUND
② BLITHE

FLAP!

Dear Neven, I'll arrive today by the moon train. Aunt Mary

I KNEW THAT HANDWRITING.

IT WAS AUNT MARY'S, AND SHE WAS THE PERSON I LOVED MOST IN ALL THE WORLD. SHE HAD BEEN MY BOYHOOD'S IDOL...

"YOU KNOW IT'S BAD FOR YOUR HEALTH!"

HUF!!

...I BECAME CALMLY, ADAMANTINELY INDIFFERENT TO HER OBJECTIONS, AND THE ONE ALLOY THAT WAS ABLE TO MAR MY ENJOYMENT OF MY AUNT'S SOCIETY...

KAFF! KAFF!

MATURITY HAD NOT BEEN ABLE TO DISLODGE HER FROM HER PEDESTAL, DESPITE HER CONTINUED DISAPPROVAL OF MY PERNICIOUS HABIT...

BUT ALL THINGS HAVE THEIR LIMIT IN THIS WORLD... I WAS GRATEFUL WHEN THAT DAY ARRIVED...

...WAS GONE!

125

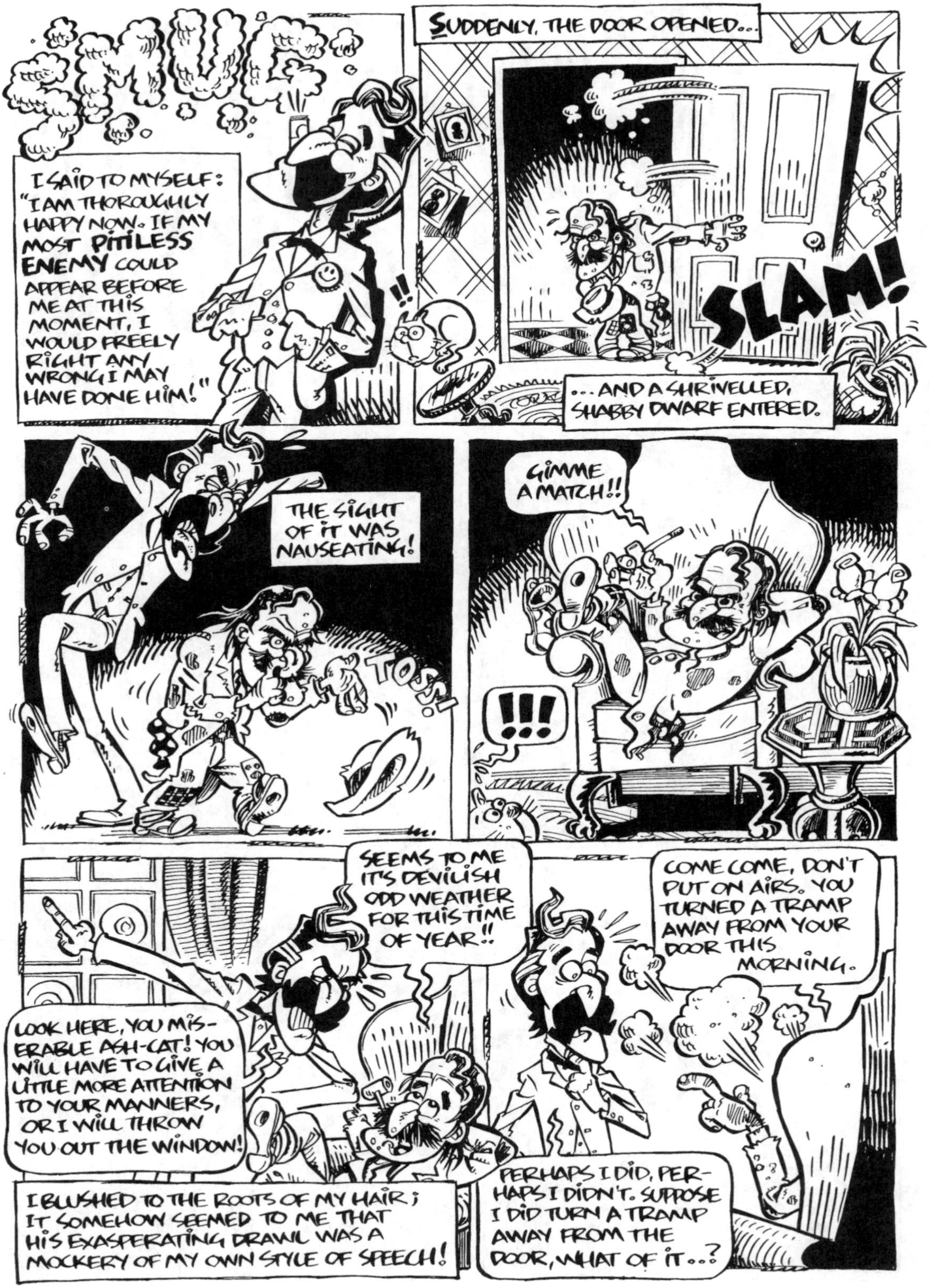
SMUG
I SAID TO MYSELF: "I AM THOROUGHLY HAPPY NOW. IF MY MOST PITILESS ENEMY COULD APPEAR BEFORE ME AT THIS MOMENT, I WOULD FREELY RIGHT ANY WRONG I MAY HAVE DONE HIM!"
!!
SUDDENLY, THE DOOR OPENED...
SLAM!
...AND A SHRIVELLED, SHABBY DWARF ENTERED.
THE SIGHT OF IT WAS NAUSEATING!
TOSS!
GIMME A MATCH!!
!!!
SEEMS TO ME IT'S DEVILISH ODD WEATHER FOR THIS TIME OF YEAR!!
LOOK HERE, YOU MISERABLE ASH-CAT! YOU WILL HAVE TO GIVE A LITTLE MORE ATTENTION TO YOUR MANNERS, OR I WILL THROW YOU OUT THE WINDOW!
I BLUSHED TO THE ROOTS OF MY HAIR; IT SOMEHOW SEEMED TO ME THAT HIS EXASPERATING DRAWL WAS A MOCKERY OF MY OWN STYLE OF SPEECH!
COME COME, DON'T PUT ON AIRS. YOU TURNED A TRAMP AWAY FROM YOUR DOOR THIS MORNING.
PERHAPS I DID, PERHAPS I DIDN'T. SUPPOSE I DID TURN A TRAMP AWAY FROM THE DOOR, WHAT OF IT..?

YOU DID, YOU LIED TO HIM!

I SAID TO THE TRAMP...

"I'M SORRY, BUT THERE IS NOTHING LEFT FROM BREAKFAST AND THE COOK HAS GONE DOWNTOWN."

SO YOU LIED TO HIM..!!

DO YOU WANT TO HAVE TO TALK ABOUT THAT POOR YOUNG WOMAN THE OTHER DAY? IT WAS RATHER **SMALL** OF YOU TO REFUSE TO READ HER MANUSCRIPT. SHE HAD COME SO FAR, TOO, AND SO HOPEFULLY. AHA! YOU FEEL ASHAMED OF IT NOW!

I TOLD THE GIRL, IN THE **KINDEST** AND **GENTLEST** WAY, THAT I COULD NOT CONSENT TO DELIVER JUDGEMENT ON ANYONE'S MANUSCRIPT...

LOOK HERE, HAVE YOU ANYTHING BETTER TO DO THAN TO PRY INTO OTHER PEOPLE'S BUSINESS? DID THE GIRL TELL YOU THAT..?

DIDDA BOM DIDDA BOM...

③

"I SAID THE GREAT PUBLIC WAS THE ONLY TRIBUNAL COMPETENT, AND THEREFORE IT MUST BE BEST TO LAY IT BEFORE THE TRIBUNAL AT THE OUTSET."

REMORSE! REMORSE! IT SEEMED TO ME THAT IT WOULD EAT THE VERY HEART OUT OF ME..!!

REMORSE
CHOMP!

SO YOU DID, YOU SAID ALL THAT... WHEN YOU SAW THE GLADNESS GO OUT OF HER EYES AND THE TEARS BEGIN... SO ASHAMED OF HER SCRIBBLING NOW, SO PROUD OF IT BEFORE...

OH PEACE! PEACE!! THESE THOUGHTS TORTURED ME ENOUGH WITHOUT YOUR COMING HERE TO FETCH THEM BACK AGAIN..!!

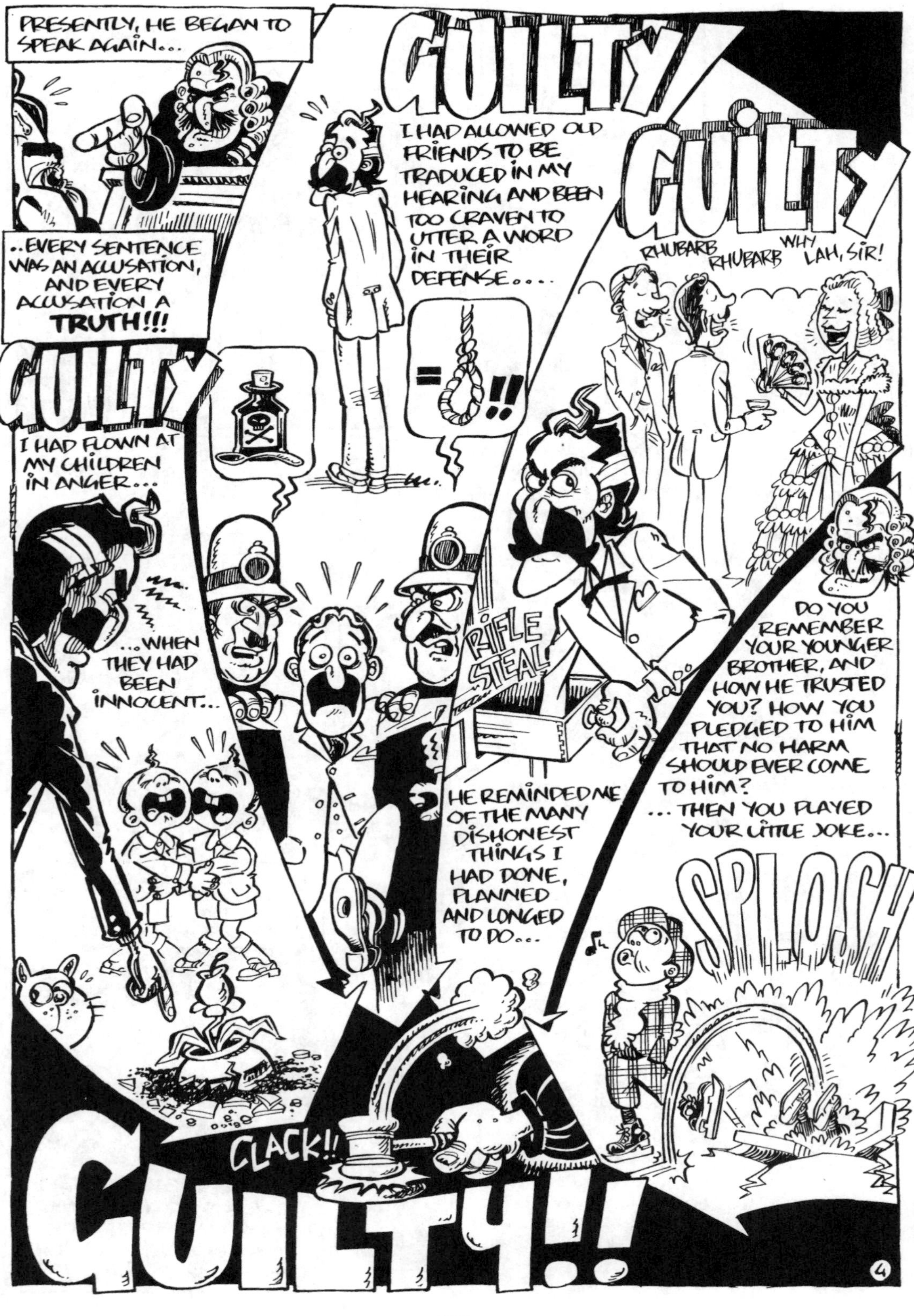
PRESENTLY, HE BEGAN TO SPEAK AGAIN...
..EVERY SENTENCE WAS AN ACCUSATION, AND EVERY ACCUSATION A TRUTH!!!
GUILTY
I HAD FLOWN AT MY CHILDREN IN ANGER...
...WHEN THEY HAD BEEN INNOCENT...
GUILTY
I HAD ALLOWED OLD FRIENDS TO BE TRADUCED IN MY HEARING AND BEEN TOO CRAVEN TO UTTER A WORD IN THEIR DEFENSE....
= !!
GUILTY
RHUBARB RHUBARB
WHY LAH, SIR!
RIFLE STEAL
HE REMINDED ME OF THE MANY DISHONEST THINGS I HAD DONE, PLANNED AND LONGED TO DO...
DO YOU REMEMBER YOUR YOUNGER BROTHER, AND HOW HE TRUSTED YOU? HOW YOU PLEDGED TO HIM THAT NO HARM SHOULD EVER COME TO HIM?
... THEN YOU PLAYED YOUR LITTLE JOKE...
SPLOSH
CLACK!!
GUILTY!!
4

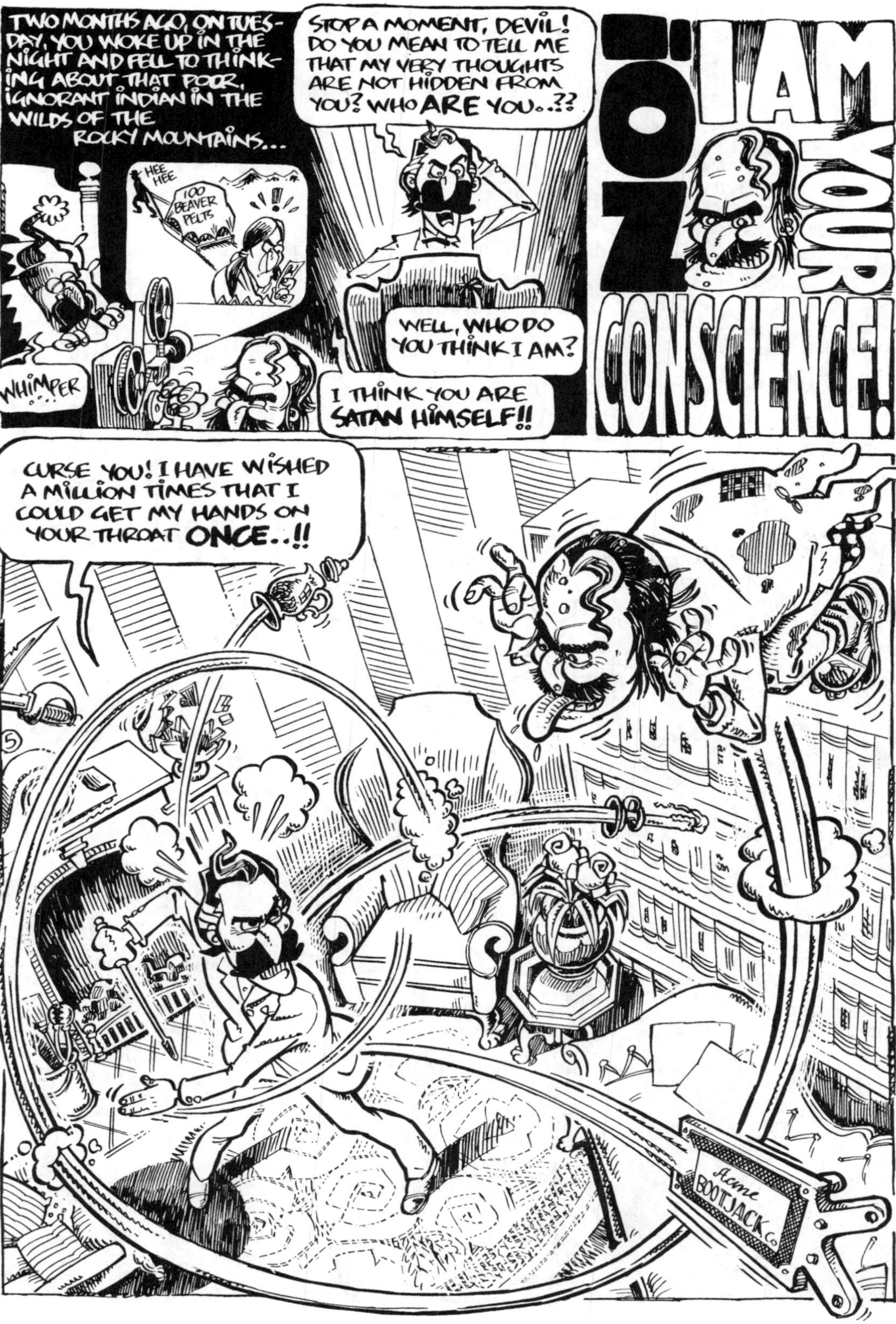
TWO MONTHS AGO, ON TUESDAY, YOU WOKE UP IN THE NIGHT AND FELL TO THINKING ABOUT THAT POOR, IGNORANT INDIAN IN THE WILDS OF THE ROCKY MOUNTAINS...
HEE HEE
100 BEAVER PELTS
WHIMPER
STOP A MOMENT, DEVIL! DO YOU MEAN TO TELL ME THAT MY VERY THOUGHTS ARE NOT HIDDEN FROM YOU? WHO ARE YOU...??
WELL, WHO DO YOU THINK I AM?
I THINK YOU ARE SATAN HIMSELF!!
"NO... I AM YOUR CONSCIENCE!
CURSE YOU! I HAVE WISHED A MILLION TIMES THAT I COULD GET MY HANDS ON YOUR THROAT ONCE..!!
Acme BOOTJACK Co.

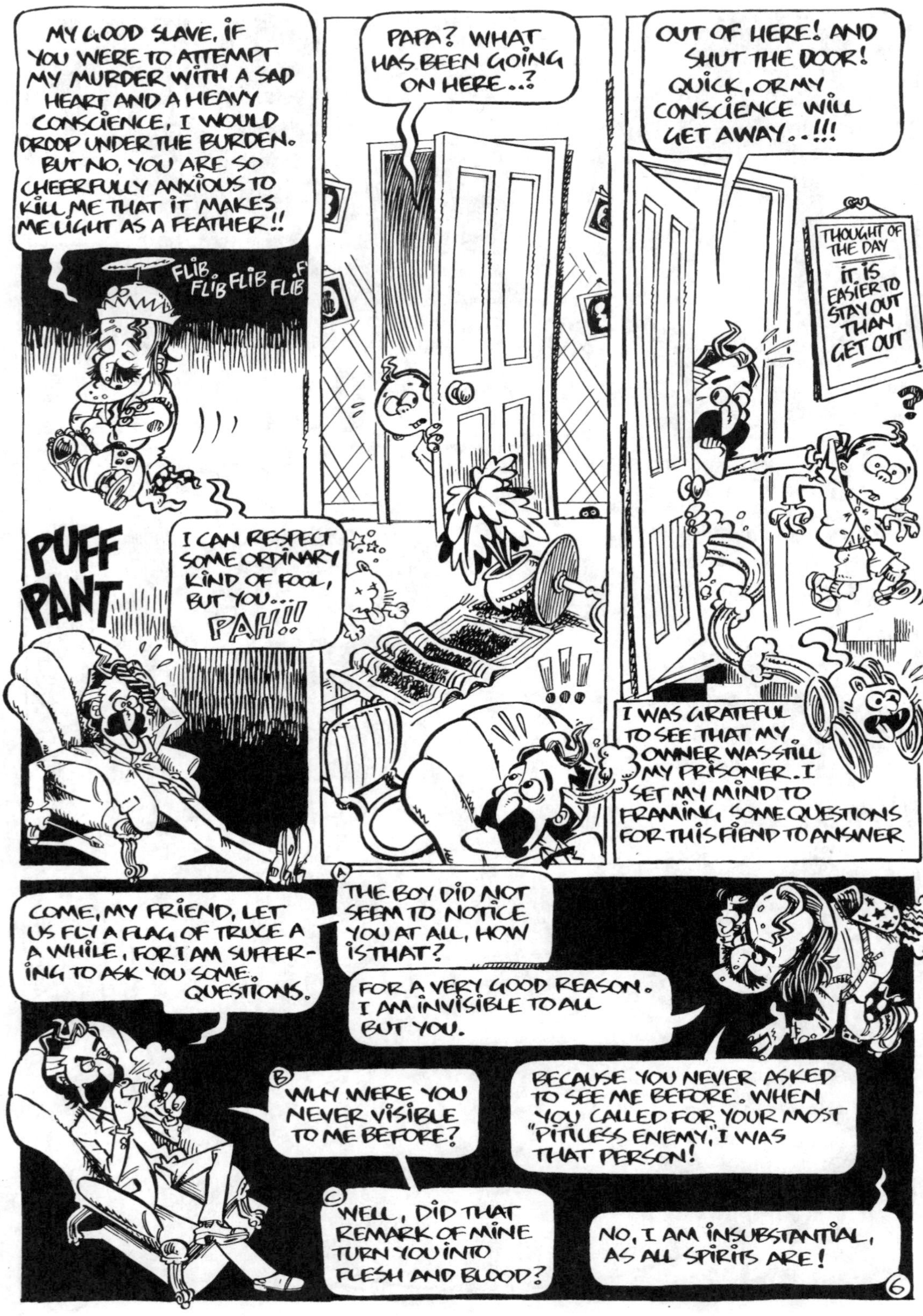
MY GOOD SLAVE, IF YOU WERE TO ATTEMPT MY MURDER WITH A SAD HEART AND A HEAVY CONSCIENCE, I WOULD DROOP UNDER THE BURDEN. BUT NO, YOU ARE SO CHEERFULLY ANXIOUS TO KILL ME THAT IT MAKES ME LIGHT AS A FEATHER!!
FLIB FLIB FLIB FLIB
PUFF PANT
I CAN RESPECT SOME ORDINARY KIND OF FOOL, BUT YOU... PAH!!
PAPA? WHAT HAS BEEN GOING ON HERE..?
!!!
OUT OF HERE! AND SHUT THE DOOR! QUICK, OR MY CONSCIENCE WILL GET AWAY..!!!
THOUGHT OF THE DAY
IT IS EASIER TO STAY OUT THAN GET OUT
?
I WAS GRATEFUL TO SEE THAT MY OWNER WAS STILL MY PRISONER. I SET MY MIND TO FRAMING SOME QUESTIONS FOR THIS FIEND TO ANSWER
COME, MY FRIEND, LET US FLY A FLAG OF TRUCE A A WHILE, FOR I AM SUFFERING TO ASK YOU SOME QUESTIONS.
A THE BOY DID NOT SEEM TO NOTICE YOU AT ALL, HOW IS THAT?
FOR A VERY GOOD REASON. I AM INVISIBLE TO ALL BUT YOU.
B WHY WERE YOU NEVER VISIBLE TO ME BEFORE?
BECAUSE YOU NEVER ASKED TO SEE ME BEFORE. WHEN YOU CALLED FOR YOUR MOST "PITILESS ENEMY," I WAS THAT PERSON!
C WELL, DID THAT REMARK OF MINE TURN YOU INTO FLESH AND BLOOD?
NO, I AM INSUBSTANTIAL, AS ALL SPIRITS ARE!
6

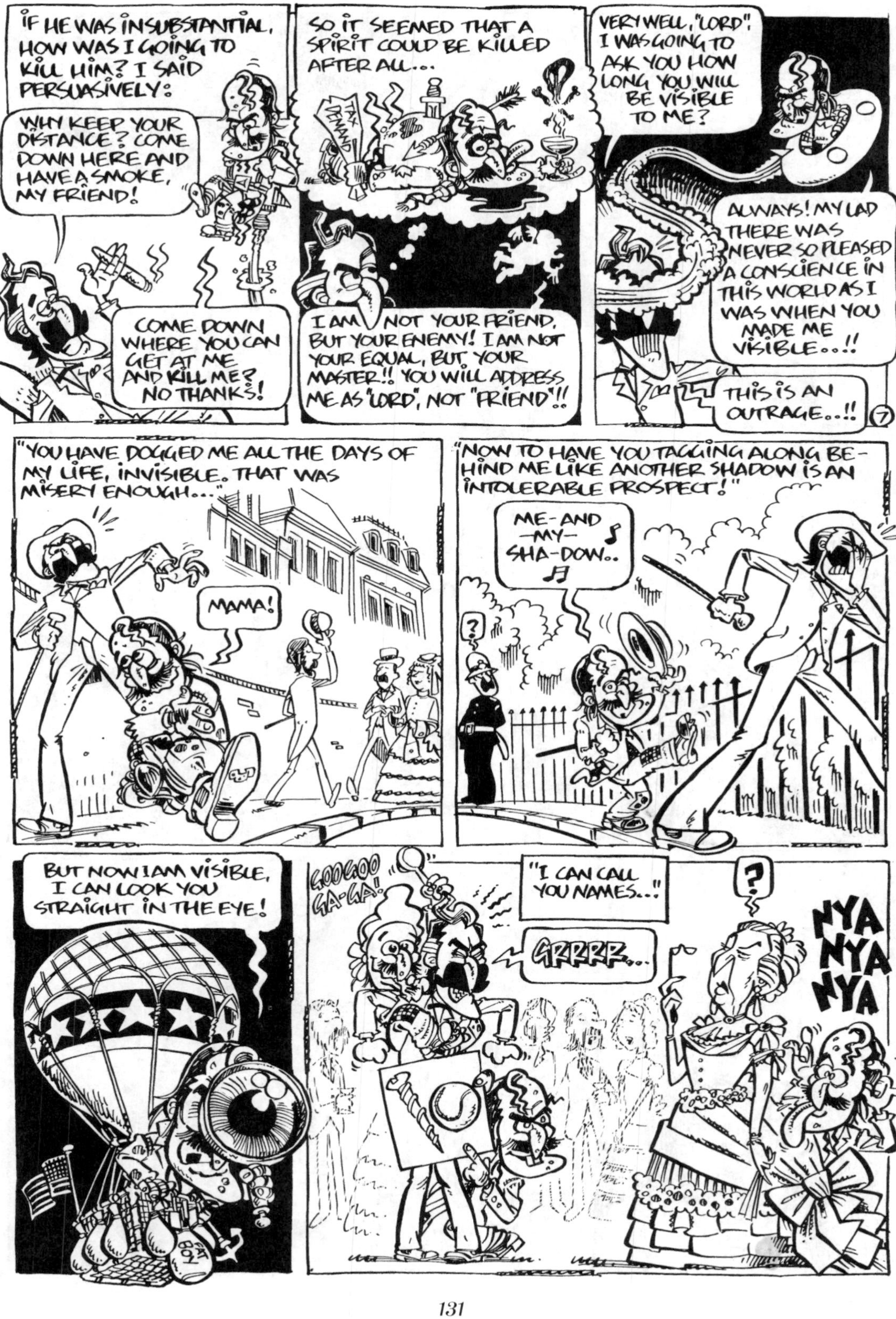
IF HE WAS INSUBSTANTIAL, HOW WAS I GOING TO KILL HIM? I SAID PERSUASIVELY:
WHY KEEP YOUR DISTANCE? COME DOWN HERE AND HAVE A SMOKE, MY FRIEND!
COME DOWN WHERE YOU CAN GET AT ME AND KILL ME? NO THANKS!
SO IT SEEMED THAT A SPIRIT COULD BE KILLED AFTER ALL...
TAX DEMAND
I AM NOT YOUR FRIEND, BUT YOUR ENEMY! I AM NOT YOUR EQUAL, BUT YOUR MASTER!! YOU WILL ADDRESS ME AS "LORD", NOT "FRIEND"!!
VERY WELL, "LORD". I WAS GOING TO ASK YOU HOW LONG YOU WILL BE VISIBLE TO ME?
ALWAYS! MY LAD THERE WAS NEVER SO PLEASED A CONSCIENCE IN THIS WORLD AS I WAS WHEN YOU MADE ME VISIBLE..!!
THIS IS AN OUTRAGE..!!
"YOU HAVE DOGGED ME ALL THE DAYS OF MY LIFE, INVISIBLE. THAT WAS MISERY ENOUGH..."
MAMA!
"NOW TO HAVE YOU TAGGING ALONG BEHIND ME LIKE ANOTHER SHADOW IS AN INTOLERABLE PROSPECT!"
ME-AND -MY- SHA-DOW..
?
BUT NOW I AM VISIBLE, I CAN LOOK YOU STRAIGHT IN THE EYE!
FAT BOY
GOOGOO GA-GA!
"I CAN CALL YOU NAMES..."
GRRRRR...
?
NYA NYA NYA

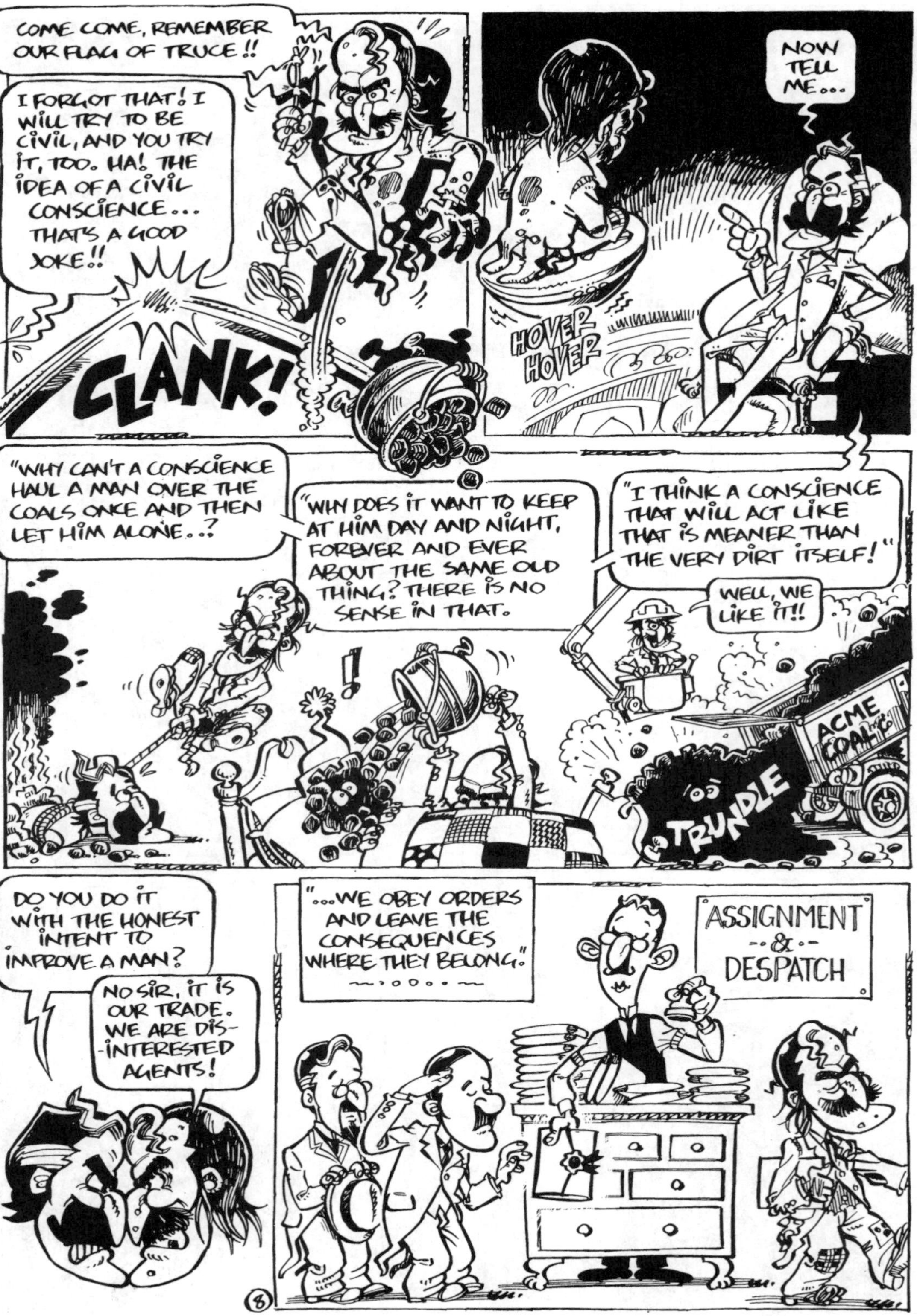
COME COME, REMEMBER OUR FLAG OF TRUCE!!
I FORGOT THAT! I WILL TRY TO BE CIVIL, AND YOU TRY IT, TOO. HA! THE IDEA OF A CIVIL CONSCIENCE... THAT'S A GOOD JOKE!!
CLANK!
NOW TELL ME...
HOVER HOVER
"WHY CAN'T A CONSCIENCE HAUL A MAN OVER THE COALS ONCE AND THEN LET HIM ALONE..?
"WHY DOES IT WANT TO KEEP AT HIM DAY AND NIGHT, FOREVER AND EVER ABOUT THE SAME OLD THING? THERE IS NO SENSE IN THAT.
"I THINK A CONSCIENCE THAT WILL ACT LIKE THAT IS MEANER THAN THE VERY DIRT ITSELF!"
WELL, WE LIKE IT!!
!
ACME COAL
TRUNDLE
DO YOU DO IT WITH THE HONEST INTENT TO IMPROVE A MAN?
NO SIR, IT IS OUR TRADE. WE ARE DIS-INTERESTED AGENTS!
"...WE OBEY ORDERS AND LEAVE THE CONSEQUENCES WHERE THEY BELONG."
ASSIGNMENT & DESPATCH
8

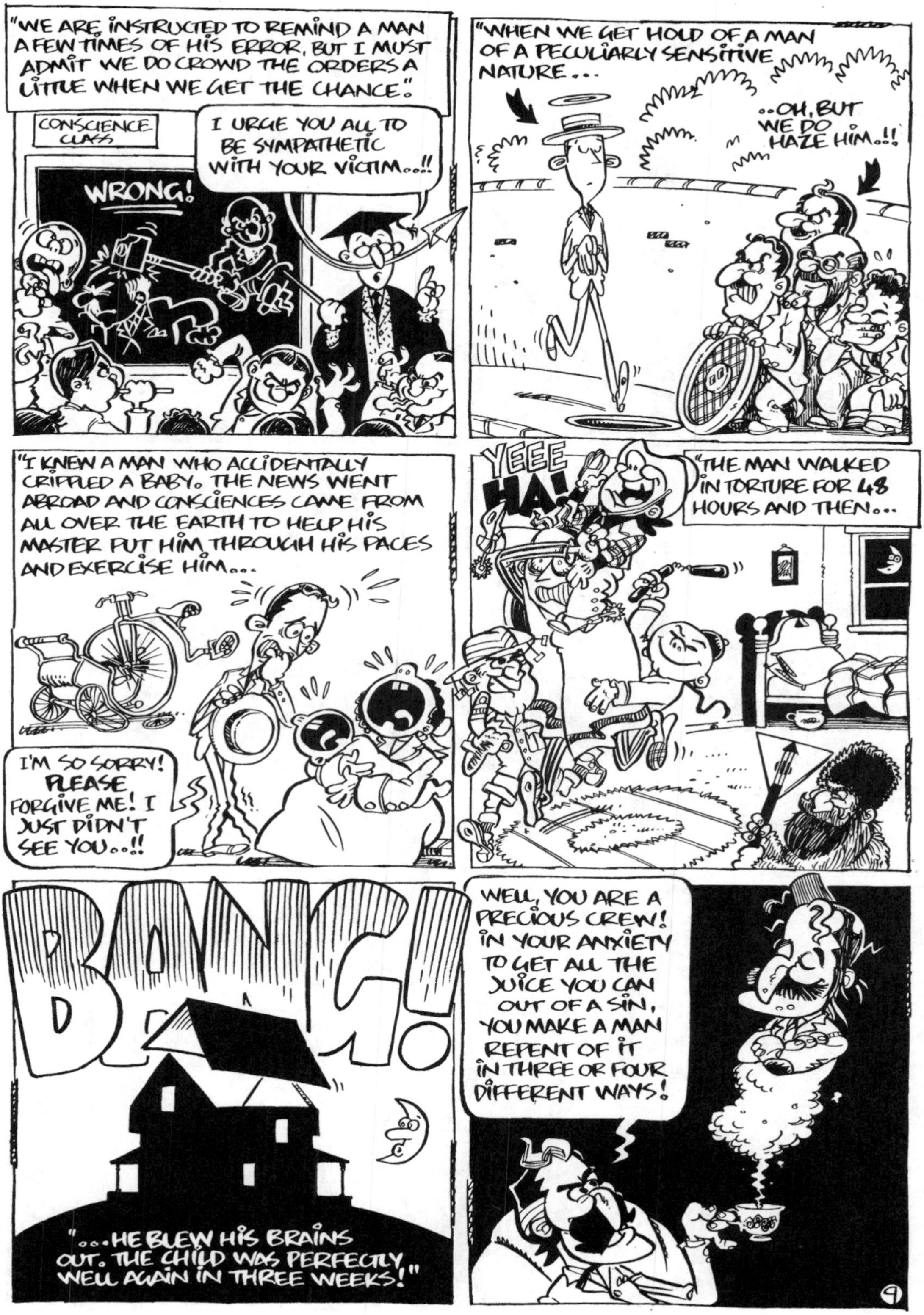
"WE ARE INSTRUCTED TO REMIND A MAN A FEW TIMES OF HIS ERROR, BUT I MUST ADMIT WE DO CROWD THE ORDERS A LITTLE WHEN WE GET THE CHANCE."
CONSCIENCE CLASS
I URGE YOU ALL TO BE SYMPATHETIC WITH YOUR VICTIM...!!
WRONG!
"WHEN WE GET HOLD OF A MAN OF A PECULIARLY SENSITIVE NATURE...
..OH, BUT WE DO HAZE HIM..!!
"I KNEW A MAN WHO ACCIDENTALLY CRIPPLED A BABY. THE NEWS WENT ABROAD AND CONSCIENCES CAME FROM ALL OVER THE EARTH TO HELP HIS MASTER PUT HIM THROUGH HIS PACES AND EXERCISE HIM...
I'M SO SORRY! PLEASE FORGIVE ME! I JUST DIDN'T SEE YOU..!!
YEEE HA!
"THE MAN WALKED IN TORTURE FOR 48 HOURS AND THEN...
BANG!
"...HE BLEW HIS BRAINS OUT. THE CHILD WAS PERFECTLY WELL AGAIN IN THREE WEEKS!"
WELL, YOU ARE A PRECIOUS CREW! IN YOUR ANXIETY TO GET ALL THE JUICE YOU CAN OUT OF A SIN, YOU MAKE A MAN REPENT OF IT IN THREE OR FOUR DIFFERENT WAYS!
9

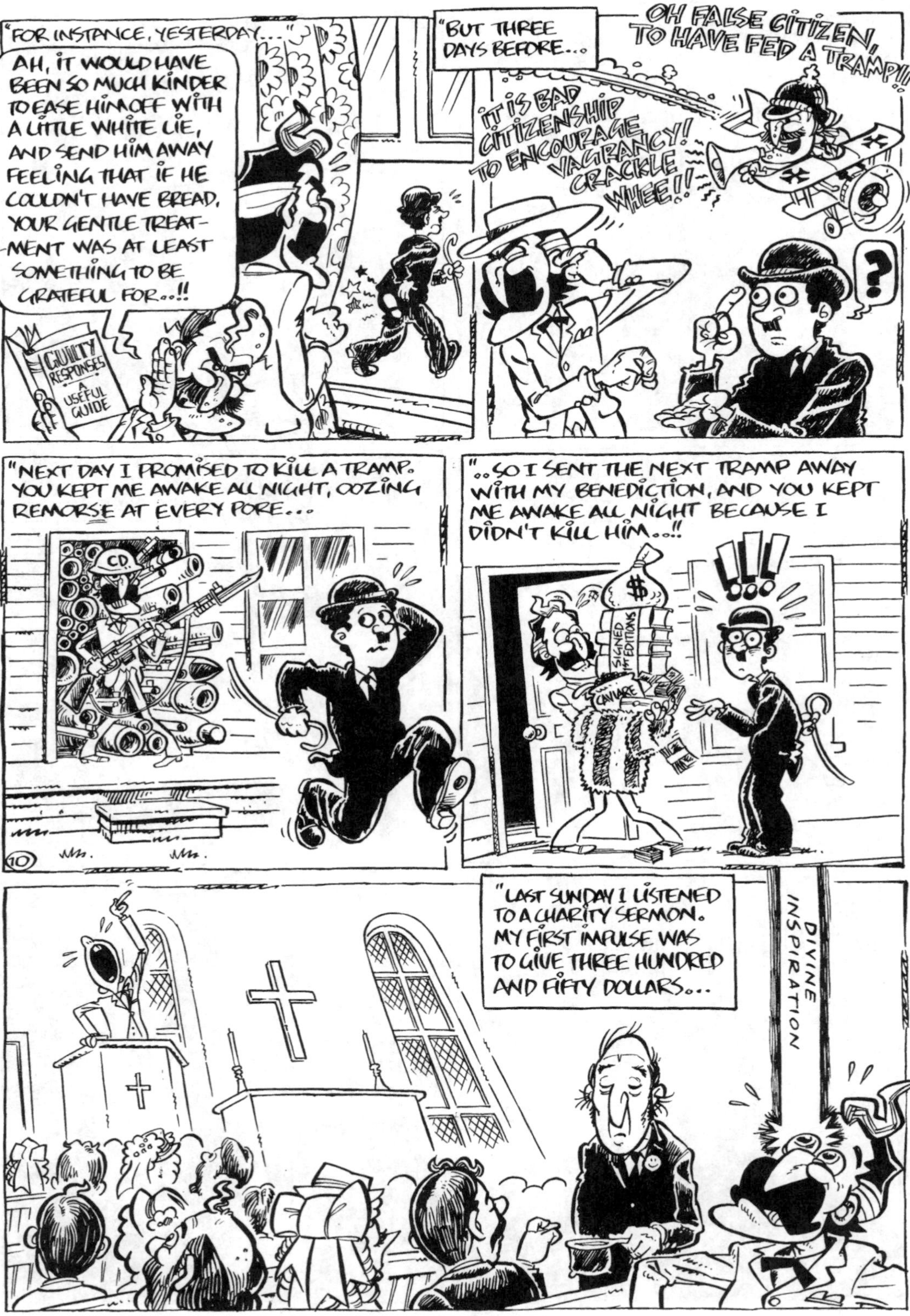
"FOR INSTANCE, YESTERDAY..."
AH, IT WOULD HAVE BEEN SO MUCH KINDER TO EASE HIM OFF WITH A LITTLE WHITE LIE, AND SEND HIM AWAY FEELING THAT IF HE COULDN'T HAVE BREAD, YOUR GENTLE TREAT-MENT WAS AT LEAST SOMETHING TO BE GRATEFUL FOR...!!
GUILTY RESPONSES A USEFUL GUIDE
"BUT THREE DAYS BEFORE...
OH FALSE CITIZEN, TO HAVE FED A TRAMP!!
IT IS BAD CITIZENSHIP TO ENCOURAGE VAGRANCY! CRACKLE WHEE!!
?
"NEXT DAY I PROMISED TO KILL A TRAMP. YOU KEPT ME AWAKE ALL NIGHT, OOZING REMORSE AT EVERY PORE...
CD
"...SO I SENT THE NEXT TRAMP AWAY WITH MY BENEDICTION, AND YOU KEPT ME AWAKE ALL NIGHT BECAUSE I DIDN'T KILL HIM...!!
$
SIGNED 1st EDITIONS
CAVIARE
!!!
"LAST SUNDAY I LISTENED TO A CHARITY SERMON. MY FIRST IMPULSE WAS TO GIVE THREE HUNDRED AND FIFTY DOLLARS...
DIVINE INSPIRATION

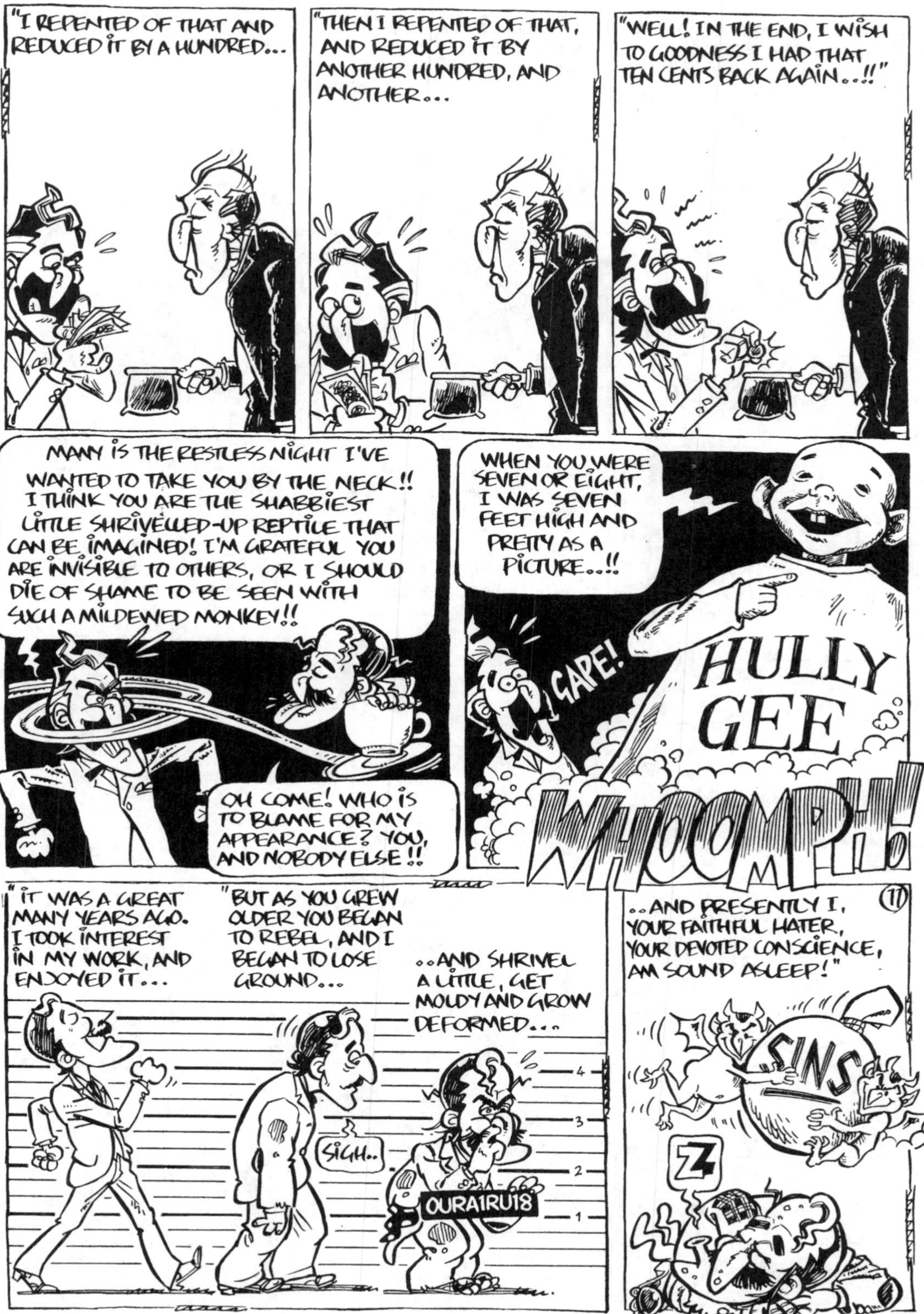
"I REPENTED OF THAT AND REDUCED IT BY A HUNDRED...
"THEN I REPENTED OF THAT, AND REDUCED IT BY ANOTHER HUNDRED, AND ANOTHER...
"WELL! IN THE END, I WISH TO GOODNESS I HAD THAT TEN CENTS BACK AGAIN..!!"
MANY IS THE RESTLESS NIGHT I'VE WANTED TO TAKE YOU BY THE NECK!! I THINK YOU ARE THE SHABBIEST LITTLE SHRIVELLED-UP REPTILE THAT CAN BE IMAGINED! I'M GRATEFUL YOU ARE INVISIBLE TO OTHERS, OR I SHOULD DIE OF SHAME TO BE SEEN WITH SUCH A MILDEWED MONKEY!!
OH COME! WHO IS TO BLAME FOR MY APPEARANCE? YOU, AND NOBODY ELSE!!
WHEN YOU WERE SEVEN OR EIGHT, I WAS SEVEN FEET HIGH AND PRETTY AS A PICTURE..!!
GAPE!
HULLY GEE
WHOOMPH!
"IT WAS A GREAT MANY YEARS AGO. I TOOK INTEREST IN MY WORK, AND ENJOYED IT...
"BUT AS YOU GREW OLDER YOU BEGAN TO REBEL, AND I BEGAN TO LOSE GROUND...
..AND SHRIVEL A LITTLE, GET MOLDY AND GROW DEFORMED...
SIGH..
4
3
2
1
..AND PRESENTLY I, YOUR FAITHFUL HATER, YOUR DEVOTED CONSCIENCE, AM SOUND ASLEEP!"
11
SINS
Z

I WISH I HAD KNOWN THIS SOME THIRTY YEARS AGO — I SHOULD HAVE TURNED MY PARTICULAR ATTENTION TO SIN! BY THIS TIME I SHOULD NOT ONLY HAVE HAD YOU PERMANENTLY ASLEEP...

"... BUT REDUCED TO THE SIZE OF A HOMEOPATHIC PILL! I WOULD FEED YOU TO A YELLOW DOG...!!"

FIDO! HERE BOY! I HAVE SOMETHING FOR YOU..!

HELP ME! HELLPP MEEEE..!!

YIP!

DO YOU KNOW A GOOD MANY CONSCIENCES?

PLENTY OF THEM!

COULD YOU BRING THEM HERE?

NO!

WOULD THEY BE VISIBLE TO ME?

NO!

TELL ME ABOUT MY NEIGHBOUR THOMPSON'S CONSCIENCE!

I KNEW HIM WHEN HE WAS ELEVEN FEET HIGH!

..AS TO HIS PRESENT SIZE, ..WELL, HE SLEEPS IN A CIGAR BOX!!

DO YOU KNOW ROBINSON'S CONSCIENCE?

YES, HE IS SHAPELY AND COMELY..!!

DO YOU KNOW TOM SMITH'S CONSCIENCE?

RING RING RING RING RING RING RING

HE IS THIRTY-SEVEN FEET HIGH AND NEVER SLEEPS. HE IS THE PRESIDENT OF THE NEW ENGLAND CONSCIENCE CLUB. HE CAN MAKE POOR SMITH IMAGINE THAT THE MOST INNOCENT LITTLE THING HE DOES IS AN ODIOUS SIN!

SMITH IS THE NOBLEST AND PUREST MAN. ONLY A CONSCIENCE COULD FIND PLEASURE IN HEAPING AGONY UPON A SPIRIT LIKE THAT..!

YOU KNOW MY AUNT MARY'S CONSCIENCE?

I HAVE SEEN HER AT A DISTANCE. SHE LIVES IN THE OPEN AIR, BE-CAUSE NO DOOR IS LARGE ENOUGH TO ADMIT HER!!

I CAN BELIEVE THAT! DO YOU KNOW THE CONSCIENCE OF THAT PUBLISHER WHO STOLE SOME SKETCHES OF MINE?

THE TINIEST CON-SCIENCE IN THE WORLD!!

YES, HE HAS A WIDE FAME. HE WAS EXHIBITED AT A SHOW A MONTH AGO. THE MANAGE-MENT COULD ONLY PROVIDE A MICRO-SCOPE WITH A MAGNIFYING POWER OF THIRTY THOUSAND DIAMETERS, SO NO-BODY GOT TO SEE HIM! THERE WAS GENERAL DISSATISFACTION!!

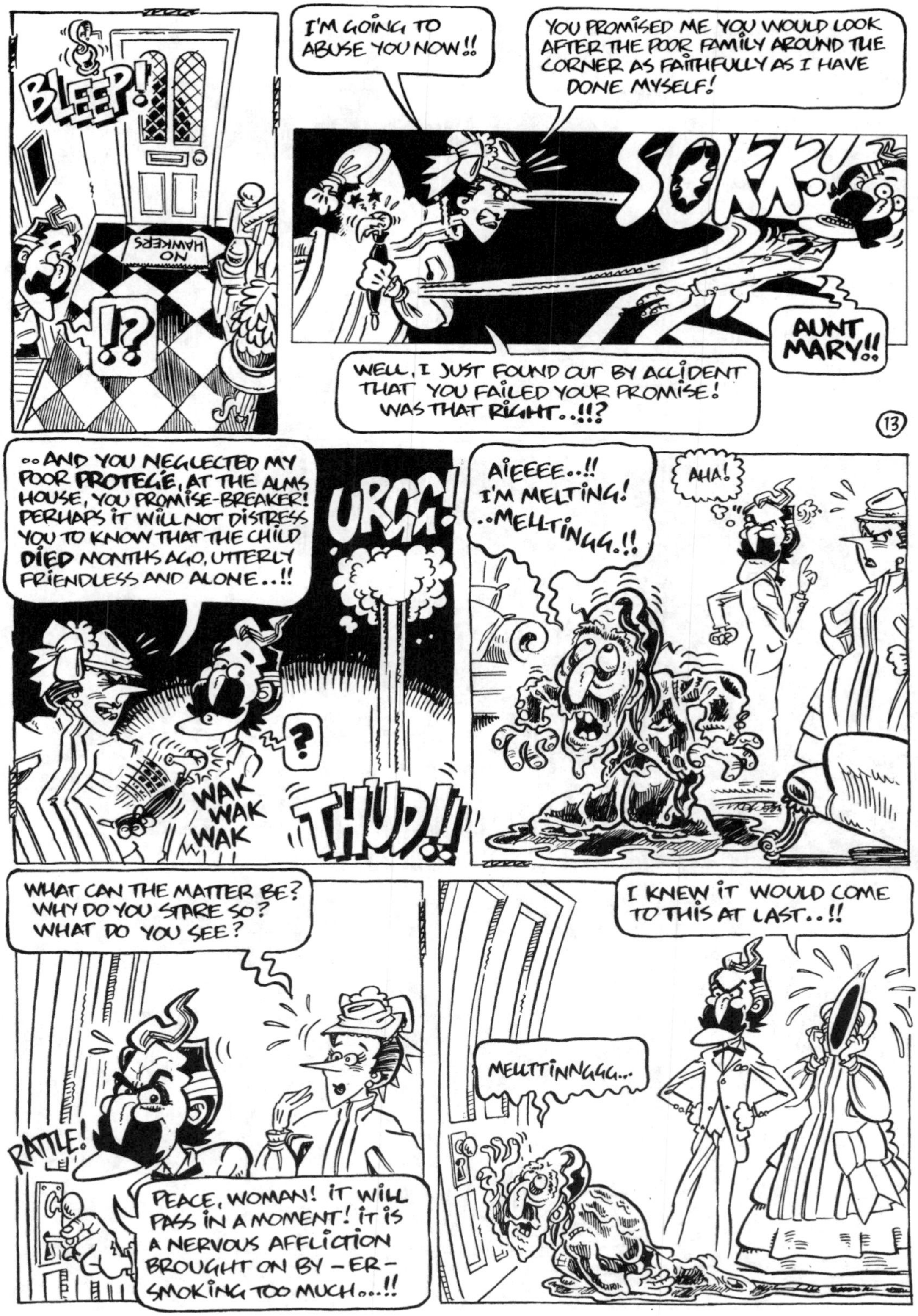
BLEEP!
NO HAWKERS
!?
I'M GOING TO ABUSE YOU NOW!!
YOU PROMISED ME YOU WOULD LOOK AFTER THE POOR FAMILY AROUND THE CORNER AS FAITHFULLY AS I HAVE DONE MYSELF!
SOKK!
AUNT MARY!!
WELL, I JUST FOUND OUT BY ACCIDENT THAT YOU FAILED YOUR PROMISE! WAS THAT RIGHT..!!?
13
..AND YOU NEGLECTED MY POOR PROTEGE, AT THE ALMS HOUSE, YOU PROMISE-BREAKER! PERHAPS IT WILL NOT DISTRESS YOU TO KNOW THAT THE CHILD DIED MONTHS AGO, UTTERLY FRIENDLESS AND ALONE..!!
URGG!
?
WAK WAK WAK
THUD!!
AIEEEE..!! I'M MELTING! ..MELLTINGG.!!
AHA!
WHAT CAN THE MATTER BE? WHY DO YOU STARE SO? WHAT DO YOU SEE?
RATTLE!
PEACE, WOMAN! IT WILL PASS IN A MOMENT! IT IS A NERVOUS AFFLICTION BROUGHT ON BY - ER - SMOKING TOO MUCH...!!
I KNEW IT WOULD COME TO THIS AT LAST..!!
MELLTTINNGGG...

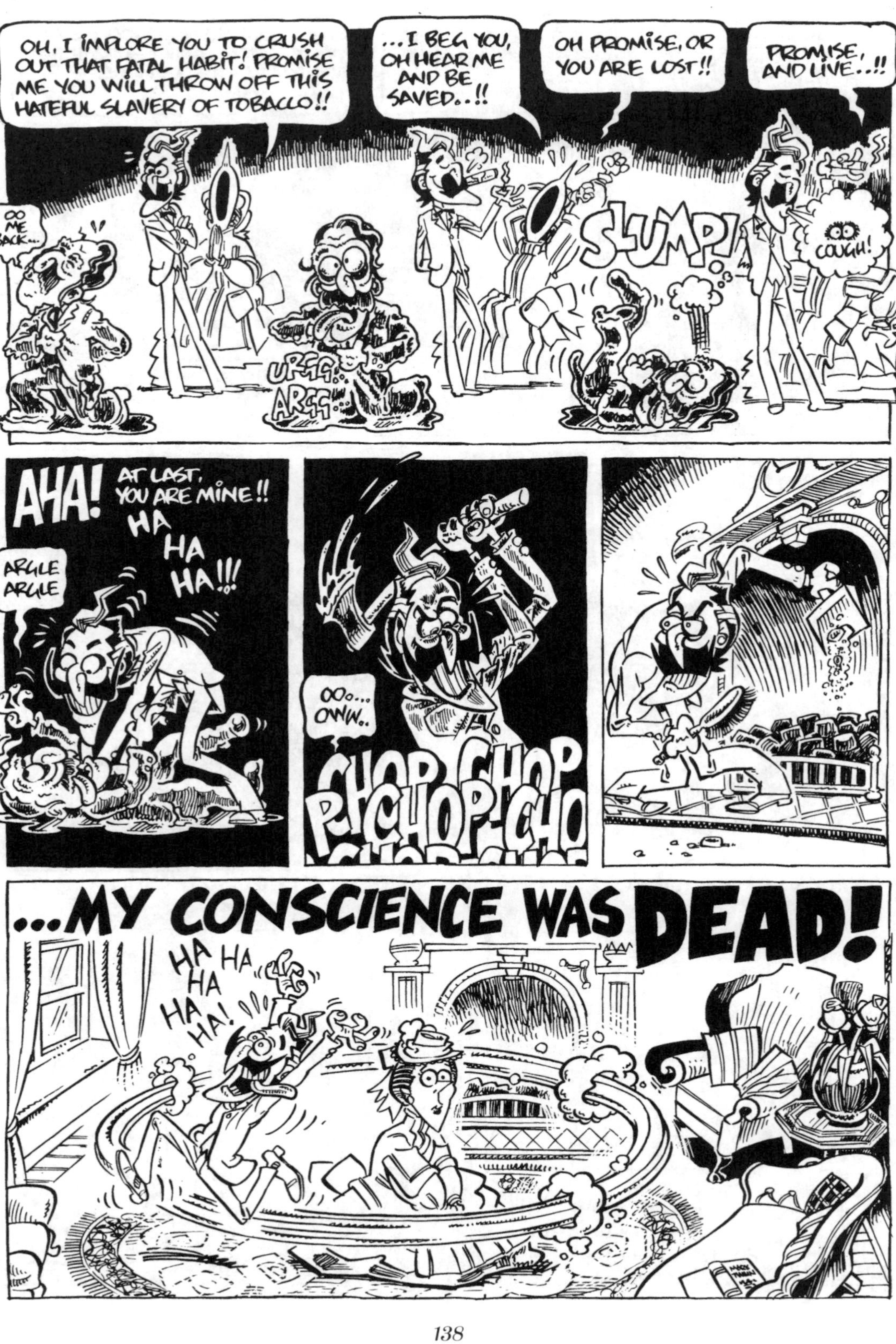
OH, I IMPLORE YOU TO CRUSH OUT THAT FATAL HABIT! PROMISE ME YOU WILL THROW OFF THIS HATEFUL SLAVERY OF TOBACCO!!
...I BEG YOU, OH HEAR ME AND BE SAVED..!!
OH PROMISE, OR YOU ARE LOST!!
PROMISE, AND LIVE..!!
OO ME BACK...
URGG!.. ARGG!..
SLUMP!
COUGH!
AHA!
AT LAST, YOU ARE MINE!! HA HA HA!!!
ARGLE ARGLE
OO... OWW..
CHOP CHOP CHOP-CHOP-CHO
...MY CONSCIENCE WAS DEAD!
HA HA HA HA HA!

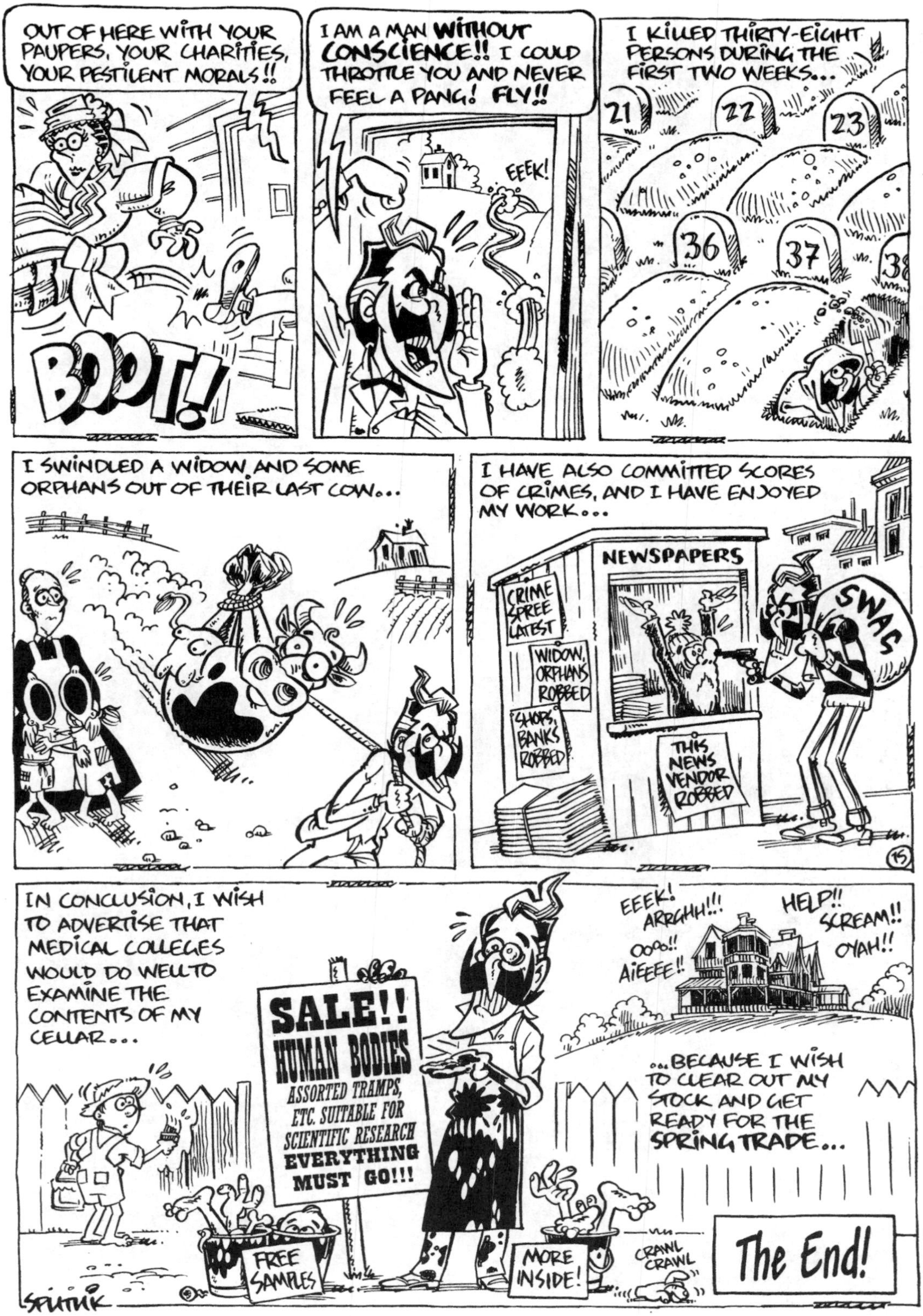
OUT OF HERE WITH YOUR PAUPERS, YOUR CHARITIES, YOUR PESTILENT MORALS!!
BOOT!
I AM A MAN WITHOUT CONSCIENCE!! I COULD THROTTLE YOU AND NEVER FEEL A PANG! FLY!!
EEEK!
I KILLED THIRTY-EIGHT PERSONS DURING THE FIRST TWO WEEKS...
21
22
23
36
37
38
I SWINDLED A WIDOW AND SOME ORPHANS OUT OF THEIR LAST COW...
I HAVE ALSO COMMITTED SCORES OF CRIMES, AND I HAVE ENJOYED MY WORK...
NEWSPAPERS
CRIME SPREE LATEST
WIDOW, ORPHANS ROBBED
SHOPS, BANKS ROBBED
THIS NEWS VENDOR ROBBED
SWAG
IN CONCLUSION, I WISH TO ADVERTISE THAT MEDICAL COLLEGES WOULD DO WELL TO EXAMINE THE CONTENTS OF MY CELLAR...
EEEK!
ARRGHH!!!
OOO!!
AIEEEE!!
HELP!!
SCREAM!!
OYAH!!
SALE!!
HUMAN BODIES
ASSORTED TRAMPS, ETC. SUITABLE FOR SCIENTIFIC RESEARCH
EVERYTHING MUST GO!!!
...BECAUSE I WISH TO CLEAR OUT MY STOCK AND GET READY FOR THE SPRING TRADE...
FREE SAMPLES
MORE INSIDE!
CRAWL CRAWL
The End!
SPUTNIK

from THE ADVENTURES OF TOM SAWYER ©2003 GEORGE SELLAS

MARK TWAIN

Born in Missouri in 1835, Samuel Langhorne Clemens took his pen name from the alert common among steamboat crews on his beloved Mississippi River for water "two fathoms deep." As a boy, he wanted to be a riverboat pilot, and became one, until the advent of the Civil War caused him, with his brother, to move to the Nevada Territory in 1861. He started as a newspaper reporter in Virginia City, and there wrote his first successful story, *The Celebrated Jumping Frog of Calaveras County*. He went on to become one of the most popular authors and humorists in American history. While today best known for what are taken as children's novels, *The Adventures of Tom Sawyer* and *The Adventures of Huckleberry Finn*, Mark Twain also authored a vast range of novels, short stories, travel books, articles, essays and satirical sketches. Failed investments and the early deaths of his wife and daughters led to an increasingly cynical view in his later writings, including *The Mysterious Stranger*. He died at his home in Connecticut at age 75.

GEORGE SELLAS (cover, page 140)

George Sellas is a freelance cartoonist and illustrator from Cheshire, Connecticut. He is a graduate of Paier College of Art in Hamden, Connecticut with a BFA in Illustration. His work has appeared in *Highlights* magazine, in *How to Draw Those Bodacious Bad Babes of Comics*, by Frank McLaughlin and Mike Gold, and in *Graphic Classics: Ambrose Bierce*. "Like all young illustrators," says George, "I'm always looking for more work to whet my artistic appetite." You can get more info and view an extensive gallery of his illustrations at www.georgesellas.com.

KEVIN ATKINSON (pages 1, 47)

"I've lived in Texas my whole life with the exception of 1985–1988 when I went to New Jersey to study with [famed comics artist and teacher] Joe Kubert," says Kevin. Since then he has done short stories and full-length comics for various publishers. He wrote and drew two series, *Snarl* and *Planet 29* and collaborated on another, *Rogue Satellite Comics*, which climaxed with a guest appearance by The Flaming Carrot. Lately he's inked *The Tick* comics and illustrated Drew Edward's *Halloween Man*. More of Kevin's art can be seen at www.meobeco.com/pulptoons/index.htm.

DAN O'NEILL (page 2)

In 1963 Dan O'Neill dropped out of college and started his comic strip *Odd Bodkins* for the *San Francisco Chronicle*. For seven years O'Neill proceeded to entertain readers and offend editors before finally being fired. These strips are collected in two books, *Hear the Sound of My Feet Walking Drown the Sound of My Voice Talking* and *The Collective Unconscience of Odd Bodkins*. In 1970, at the height of the underground comix movement, O'Neill met four cartoonists who would form the core of his infamous comics collective, The Air Pirates: Ted Richards, Gary Hallgren, Bobby London and Shary Flenniken. They produced comics which consisted largely of satires of Disney cartoon characters. O'Neill's intent was to provoke a reaction from the Disney empire and in 1971 he succeeded. The highly-publicized court case, which dragged out for nine years, is detailed in Bob Levin's *The Pirates and The Mouse*. Dan returned to newspaper comics with his *Dan O'Neill* strip that continues today in *The San Francisco Bay Guardian* and other papers. His work also appears in *Graphic Classics: H.G. Wells* and *Graphic Classics: Ambrose Bierce*.

WILLIAM L. BROWN (pages 3, 96)

Political cartoonist and illustrator William L. Brown is the author of *President Bill, A Graphic Epic*, and the continuing cartoon *Citizen Bill*. His illustration clients include *The Washington Post*, *The Wall Street Journal*, *Slate* online magazine, *The Los Angeles Times* and *The Progressive*. He works in scratchboard, digitally adding color and grey tones. He cites as influences William Morris, John Held, Jr., and the British cartoonist Giles. Bill lives in Takoma Park, Maryland, a suburb of Washington, D.C., with his wife and two children. See more of his work at www.wmlbrown.com.

MARK DANCEY (page 4)

Mark Dancey was born in Ann Arbor, Michigan in 1963. "For no good reason," Mark co-founded the satirical and highly influential *Motorbooty Magazine* in the late 1980s and filled its pages with his comics and illustrations. As a member of rock band Big Chief during the 1990s he got a lock on the position of band propagandist and subsequently produced all manner of CD covers, T-shirt designs, backdrops and posters for that outfit. Having extricated himself from the world of rock, Mark now lives in Detroit, where he produces painstaking works in oil and prints silk-screened posters under the aegis of his company, Illuminado.com.

RICK GEARY (page 6)

Rick is best known for his thirteen years as a contributor to *The National Lampoon*. His work has also appeared in Marvel, DC, and Dark Horse comics, *Rolling Stone*, *Mad*, *Heavy Metal*, *Disney Adventures*, *The Los Angeles Times*, and *The New York Times Book Review*. He is a regular cartoonist in *Rosebud*. Rick has written and illustrated five children's books and published a collection of his comics, *Housebound with Rick Geary*. The fifth volume in his continuing book series *A Treasury of*

Victorian Murder is *The Beast of Chicago* (NBM Publishing, 2003). More of Rick's work has appeared in the *Graphic Classics* anthologies *Edgar Allan Poe*, *Arthur Conan Doyle*, *H.G. Wells*, *H.P. Lovecraft*, *Jack London* and *Ambrose Bierce*. You can also view his art at www.rickgeary.com.

MILTON KNIGHT (page 42)

Milton Knight claims he started drawing, painting and creating his own attempts at comic books and animation at age two. "I've never formed a barrier between fine art and cartooning," says Milt. "Growing up, I treasured Chinese watercolors, Breughel, Charlie Brown and Terrytoons equally." His work has appeared in magazines including *Heavy Metal*, *High Times*, *National Lampoon* and *Nickelodeon Magazine*, and he has illustrated record covers, posters, candy packaging and T-shirts, and occasionally exhibited his paintings. Labor on *Ninja Turtles* comics allowed him to get up a grubstake to move to the West Coast in 1991, where he became an animator and director on *Felix the Cat* cartoons. Milt's comics titles include *Midnite the Rebel Skunk*, *Hinkley*, and *Slug and Ginger* and *Hugo*. He has appeared in *Graphic Classics: H.G. Wells*, *Graphic Classics: Jack London* and *Graphic Classics: Ambrose Bierce*, and is now working on an adaptation of *Never Bet the Devil Your Head* for the revised second edition of *Graphic Classics: Edgar Allan Poe*. Check for the latest news at www.miltonknight.net.

EVERT GERADTS (page 59, back cover)

Evert Geradts is a Dutch comics artist now living in Toulouse, France. One of the founders of the Dutch underground comix scene, he started the influential magazine *Tante Leny Presents*, in which appeared his first *Sailears & Susie* stories. He is a disciple of Carl Barks, whom he names "the Aesop of the 20th century." Over the years Geradts has written about a thousand stories for Dutch comics of Donald Duck and other Disney characters. He also writes stories for the popular comic series *Sjors & Sjimmie* and *De Muziekbuurters*. He now does all his art on computer, developing the supple vector style he applies to his "kids in space" series *Kos & Mo*. "All my life I have been waiting for the arrival of personal computers with good illustration programs," says Evert. "Adobe Illustrator and my Mac have set me free from the traditional drawing style where the obligatory black outline was always the frontier between color and form."

JACKIE SMITH (page 64)

Jackie Smith comes from Sheffield, in northern England. She originally trained as an animator and has drawn comics since the late 1970s. She's been a T-shirt designer, graphic artist and Youth Arts Worker and has been a freelance cartoonist, writer and illustrator since 1980. Her best work has appeared in *Knockabout Comics*, as well as *Graphic Classics: Ambrose Bierce*. Other long-term contracts have been with *Big Mags* and *Myatt McFarlane*. Jackie says her most revelatory moment was being invited to exhibit at the World Comics Convention in Angouleme, France, which she called "a mind-broadening experience." She also takes comics and illustration into schools and has used *Graphic Classics* in her work with excluded teenagers. Jackie draws caricatures and portraits at fairs and sneaks off to the wild peaks to paint landscapes. Present projects include a graphic novel and a series of portraits of scary teenagers.

DAN E. BURR (page 66)

Together with author James Vance, Dan Burr is a winner of the comic industry's Eisner and Harvey awards for the graphic novel *Kings In Disguise*. Dan has also produced a number of historical comics for the DC/Paradox *Big Book* series, and he has worked extensively for Golden Books and other publishers doing illustrations for children's educational materials. *The Disappearance of Ambrose Bierce*, in *Graphic Classics: Ambrose Bierce*, is an homage by Dan and writer Mort Castle to the style of *Mad* magazine's great Will Elder. Of late, Dan has been concentrating on portraiture and caricature work, a sampling of which can be viewed at www.kookykool.com.

ANTON EMDIN (page 68)

Claiming to live on a diet of squirrels, beer, and puppy drool, Anton produces illustrations and comic strips from his home studio in Sydney, Australia. His work has appeared in various magazines, websites, comics, and books as well as adorning posters, T-shirts and the occasional skin canvas. Aside from the necessary commercial work, Anton contributes weirdo comic art to underground comix anthologies, both in Australia and overseas, as well as self-publishing his own mini-comic, the now-sleeping ("soon, my pretties") *Cruel World*. You can find more of Anton's work on the cover of *Graphic Classics: Ambrose Bierce*, in *Graphic Classics: Bram Stoker*, and online at www.antongraphics.com.

LANCE TOOKS (page 81)

As an animator for fifteen years, as well as a comics artist, Lance Tooks' work has appeared in more than a hundred television commercials, films and music videos. He has self-published the comic books *Danger Funnies*, *Divided by Infinity* and *Muthafucka*. His comics have appeared in *Zuzu*, *Shade*, *Vibe*, *Girltalk*, *World War 3 Illustrated*, *Floaters*, *Pure Friction*, the Italian magazine *Lupo Alberto*, and *Graphic*

Classics: Ambrose Bierce. He also illustrated *The Black Panthers for Beginners*, written by Herb Boyd. Lance's first graphic novel, *Narcissa* (Doubleday, 2002) was named one of the best books of 2002 by *Publisher's Weekly*. Lance recently moved from his native New York to Madrid, Spain, where he plans to "continue to do stories that are life-affirming."

LISA K. WEBER *(page 100)*

Lisa is a graduate of Parsons School of Design in New York City, where she is currently employed in the fashion industry, designing prints and characters for teenage girls' jammies, while freelancing work on children's books and character design for animation. Other projects include her "creaturized" opera posters and playing cards. Lisa provided the unique cover and illustrations for *Hop-Frog* in *Graphic Classics: Edgar Allan Poe*, and also appeared in *Graphic Classics: H.P. Lovecraft*, *Graphic Classics: Ambrose Bierce* and *Graphic Classics: Bram Stoker*. Illustrations from her in-progress book *The Shakespearean ABCs* were printed in *Rosebud 25*. More of Lisa's art can be seen online at www.creatureco.com.

SIMON GANE *(page 102)*

British artist Simon lives and works in Bath as a magazine and children's book illustrator and graphic designer. His first published strips appeared in the self-produced punk fanzine *Arnie*, and others followed in self-contained mini comics and eventually the collection *Punk Strips*. He's now completing *All Flee*, a comic to be published by Top Shelf about a "finishing school for monsters" and a four-issue series set in the Paris and New York of the 1950s for Slave Labor Graphics. "I especially enjoyed drawing *The Policeman and the Citizen* in *Graphic Classics: Ambrose Bierce*," says Simon, "because it encompasses many of my favorite themes: alcohol, police aggression, a past-times setting and a sense that whilst largely forgotten now, comics remain a peerless medium for satire." For *Is He Living or Is He Dead?*, Simon spent time sketching in Menton, the setting of the story, which contributes to the rich backgrounds. He is now at work on *Dr. Jekyll and Mr. Hyde* for *Graphic Classics: Robert Louis Stevenson*.

FLORENCE CESTAC *(page 115)*

Born in 1949, Florence Cestac studied art in Rouen and Paris. She co-founded Bonbel, an artist collective in Rouen, and in 1972 she co-founded the bookstore Futuropolis and later a publishing company with the same name. Her comic character "Harry Mickson" became the company's emblem and mascot. Cestac's work has appeared in magazines including *Ah Nana!*, *Métal Hurlant*, *Charlie Mensuel*, *Pilote* and *Chic*, and in *Graphic Classics: Ambrose Bierce*.

Her books include *Cauchemar Matinal*, *Comment Faire de la Bédé*, *La Guerre des Boutons*, *Le Démon de Midi*, *Je Veux Pas Divorcer* and *Survivre & Noël*. Her latest is *La Vie D'Artiste*, a comics autobiography published in 2002 by Dargaud.

KIRSTEN ULVE *(page 116)*

Kirsten Ulve began her career as a graphic designer and part-time illustrator in Chicago, then relocated to New York in 1996 to devote herself to illustration full time. Since then she has worked in almost every arena of the field, ranging from fashion illustration to caricatures, animated commercials to advertising art, editorial illustration to product embellishment. Her clients include *Entertainment Weekly*, *Rolling Stone*, *Cosmogirl*, *Seventeen*, *The Village Voice*, *Nickelodeon*, Mattel, Popsicle, Hasbro and Palty of Japan. She has exhibited her work at the CWC Gallery in Tokyo (August, 2000), and at Sixspace Gallery in Los Angeles (June, 2003). You can find more of her work at www.kirstenulve.com.

SHARY FLENNIKEN *(page 117)*

Shary Flenniken is a cartoonist, editor, author and screenwriter. She is best known for her irreverent comic strip *Trots & Bonnie*, about precocious pre-teens, which appeared in various underground comics and *National Lampoon*. Shary's graphic stories and comic strips have appeared in *Details*, *Premiere*, *Harvey*, and *Mad* magazines, as well as in *Graphic Classics: H.G. Wells* and *Graphic Classics: Ambrose Bierce*. Her artwork can also be seen in *When a Man Loves A Walnut*, *More Misheard Lyrics* by the "very cool" Gavin Edwards, *Nice Guys Sleep Alone* by "big-time loser" Bruce Feirstein, and *Seattle Laughs*, a "truly wonderful" book edited by Shary. She is currently teaching comedy writing and cartooning while working on a book of fairy tales and a series of novels that she claims are "not even remotely autobiographical." You can contact Shary and find out how to purchase original artwork at www.sharyflenniken.com.

TONI PAWLOWSKY *(page 118)*

Toni is both an exhibiting fine artist and a commercial illustrator. She shows her watercolors at the Fanny Garver Gallery in Madison, WI, and is represented by Langley and Associates in Chicago. Her commercial work includes numerous CD covers for the series *Music for Little People*, including two covers for Taj Mahal. She has done work for the Wisconsin Dance Ensemble and Madison Ballet. Toni lives in Madison with her three sons, Jason, Justin, and Jared. She was the featured artist in *Rosebud 17* and appears in *Graphic Classics: Edgar Allan Poe*. Her greeting cards are available at www.redoakcards.com, prints can be purchased at www.guild.com, and more art can be viewed at www.kookykool.com.

MARY FLEENER (page 119)

Besides doing comics, like her biweekly strip *Mary-Land*, autobiographical collection *Life of the Party*, and Eros title *Nipplez 'n' Tum Tum*, Los Angeles native Mary has also done illustration for magazines and books such as *Guitar Player*, *Musician*, *Spin*, *Hustler*, *The Book of Changes*, *Guitar Cookbook*, and Poppy Z. Brite's *Plastic Jesus*. Her paintings have been shown at The American Visionary Art Museum, La Luz de Jesus Gallery, and the Laguna Beach Art Museum. She is currently painting on black velvet, and makes hand-thrown ceramics. Fleener also plays bass, and sings her own tunes in a band called The Wigbillies, with her husband. She loves to surf, and walks a lot. Her website is at www.maryfleener.com.

ANNIE OWENS (page 120)

Annie was born in Alabama, "parcel posted to the Philippines," and after three years was returned to the States and educated in the San Francisco Bay area where she earned her BFA in film and video. She is a fan of old horror films, the art of Charles Addams and Edward Gorey and the writings of Roald Dahl, Edgar Allan Poe and H.P. Lovecraft, and her adaptation of *Oil of Dog* appears in *Graphic Classics: Ambrose Bierce*. Samples of Annie's comic strip *Ouchclub* can be seen at www.ouchclub.com as well as in Attaboy's comic anthology, *I Hate Cartoons, Volume II*.

LESLEY REPPETEAUX (page 121)

Lesley (aka Black Olive) is a Los Angeles-based illustrator whose work has appeared in numerous publications including *Amplifier Magazine*, *Adventure Cyclist*, *Bitch*, *Delaware Today*, *Graphic Classics: Jack London*, *Graphic Classics: Ambrose Bierce* and *Graphic Classics: Bram Stoker*. Between freelance assignments, she exhibits her paintings in galleries nationwide, and is the creative force behind *Outlook: Grim*, a spooky new comic book series published by Slave Labor Graphics. When she is "not overexerting herself or being a busy little bumblebee," she is updating her website which you can check out at www.reppeteaux.com.

SKIP WILLIAMSON (page 122)

A Chicago native, Skip Williamson began his cartooning in the alternative newspapers *The Chicago Mirror* and *The Chicago Seed*. In 1968 he produced *Bijou Funnies*, one of the earliest and longest-running underground comix titles, with Robert Crumb and Jay Lynch. During the 1970s and 1980s Williamson was an art director for what he calls "the carnal fleshpool of Hugh Hefner's *Playboy* magazine." In addition to numerous comics including *Gag Reflex*, *Naked Hostility*, *Pighead*, *Class War Comix* and *Smoot*, he has published two anthologies of his work, *Halsted Street* and *The Scum Also Rises*. Skip is now editing and assembling a 300-page anthology entitled *My Bitter Agenda*. Williamson recently moved to the Atlanta area, where he is now concentrating on painting large-scale canvases. His paintings have shown in numerous art galleries and were featured in *Rosebud 24*. His comics appear in *Graphic Classics: H.G. Wells* and *Graphic Classics: Ambrose Bierce*. You can see more of Skip's bitter agenda at www.thewilliamsongallery.bizland.com.

ANTONELLA CAPUTO (page 125)

Antonella Caputo was born and educated in Rome, Italy, and is now living in England. She has been an architect, archaeologist, art restorer, photographer, calligrapher, interior designer, theater designer, actress and theater director. Antonella's first published work was *Casa Montesi*, a weekly comic strip that appeared in *Il Journalino*. She has since written comedies for children and scripts for comics in Europe and the U.S., before joining Nick Miller as a partner in Sputnik Studios. Nick and Antonella previously collaborated in *Graphic Classics: H.G. Wells*, *Graphic Classics: Jack London* and *Graphic Classics: Ambrose Bierce*.

NICHOLAS MILLER (page 125)

The son of two artists, Nick Miller learned to draw at an early age. After leaving college, he worked as a graphic designer before a bout of chronic fatigue syndrome forced him to switch to cartooning full-time. Since then, his work has appeared in numerous adult and children's magazines as well as comics anthologies in Britain, Europe and the U.S. His weekly newspaper comics run in *The Planet on Sunday*. He shares his Lancaster, England house with two cats, a lodger and Antonella Caputo. See more of Nick's work at http://www.cat-box.net/sputnik.

TOM POMPLUN

The designer, editor and publisher of *Graphic Classics*, Tom has a background in both fine and commercial arts and a lifelong interest in comics. He designed and produced *Rosebud*, a journal of fiction, poetry and illustration, from 1993 to 2003, and in 2001 he founded *Graphic Classics*. Tom is currently working on the ninth book in the series, *Graphic Classics: Robert Louis Stevenson*, featuring *The Strange Case of Dr. Jekyll and Mr. Hyde*, scheduled for release in June 2004, as well as a completely revised and expanded edition of *Graphic Classics: Edgar Allan Poe*, due in March. It will include new comics adaptations of *The Fall of the House of Usher* and *The Cask of Amontillado*. You can see previews at www.graphicclassics.com.